"Move, move, move!" he said aloud, trying to will the airplane to get flying speed, to get off the ground, to get out of range of the guns.

If they caught him, it would mean a Mexican prison for sure. And oh God, he wouldn't be able to take that: penned up, without Bonnie, not able to be free. . . .

Finally he felt the wheels lift clear. He was flying. Ahead was a low mountain ridge, rising in front of him a mile or so off. It seemed to get higher as he struggled for altitude.

He glanced at his altimeter. He was maybe two hundred feet above the ground. Then he *felt* rather than heard the starboard engine skip a beat.

He glanced across the cockpit and out the passenger window. He couldn't see if it had been hit.

Then it missed again. He felt his heart in his throat and a sick feeling in the pit of his stomach.

Ahead the ridge was coming closer and he needed at least another two hundred feet of altitude.

CHINA
BLUE

Giles Tippette

A DELL/EMERALD BOOK

This is a work of fiction. All the characters and events
portrayed in this book are fictional, and any resemblance
to real people or incidents is purely coincidental.

Published by
Dell Publishing Co., Inc.
1 Dag Hammarskjold Plaza
New York, New York 10017

Dell ® TM 681510, Dell Publishing Co., Inc.

ISBN: 0-440-01164-7

Printed in the United States of America
First printing—April 1984

Chapter One

He awoke with the glow of the pearly grey dawn coming through the patio doors of the bedroom. He got out of bed gently, so as not to awaken Bonnie, who was sleeping curled up in a ball of sheets and looking very fragile, very pretty. On the chair was a pair of jeans that he'd taken off the night before; he put them on. Without a belt they fell loosely down around his hips. He padded barefoot down the hall and into the kitchen. There was enough first day-light to see his way, so he left the electric lights off. In the kitchen he went to the refrigerator, took out six oranges and squeezed a glass of juice. Then he took the glass and sat down at the breakfast table. He lit a cigarette.

The call from the man in New York had come the day before and it would be time to leave in less than two hours. It was a Mexico trip and it had scared Bonnie, as it always did, because her husband had been killed on a Mexico run. But then, all of the runs scared her, and had ever since she'd come to live with him. When the phone rang, he could almost see her face tense up. And it wouldn't relax until she'd found out it was a call of no consequence. The night before, he'd tried to convince her that the Mexico trip was just a milk run, as always. But, of course, she hadn't believed him, just as she never believed any of the trips were milk runs.

In a little while she'd be up and they'd laugh and joke until it was time for him to leave. Then he knew she'd sit with her fists knotted and her heart in her throat until he got back.

Well, there was nothing he could do about that. The fact was, every run scared him, too, and it was an added burden to have to convince someone else that it was safe when he knew damn good and well it wasn't.

He stubbed his cigarette out in the orange juice glass and got up and stretched. He was a tall man, a little over six feet, with wide shoulders and a gracefully deceptive way of moving. Women thought him good-looking; he'd never particularly thought so. His face suggested an easygoing nature, a softness almost, but that was belied when his eyes got hard—and they got like flint when he was confronted with something or someone that he thought wrong. His eyes were strange. They changed from blue to green to hazel, depending upon his mood. His ancestors were French, Indian and Jewish. He liked to joke that when his eyes were blue and he was in an excellent mood, he was French. They turned green, he said, when he felt Jewish. When they went hazel, it was the Indian coming out—and that was a time to be very careful.

Only it wasn't a joke.

He moved across the kitchen and stepped through the back door to go look at his horses and check on his plane.

His name was China Blue. He was thirty-four years old and he was a venture pilot, a member of a loose knit organization of some forty members who would fly anything anywhere, or anybody so long as the money was right and the job didn't smell too bad to them.

It did not matter if it was illegal. On the run to Mexico he'd be transporting in electronic products, TVs and radios and stereos, in order to avoid the duty. What made it dangerous was that the Mexican government was determined to discourage the practice, even if they had to shoot you out of the air to do it. But the money was worth it. He'd be paid a dollar a pound for all the cargo he could land in Mexico and, in the DC-3 they'd have available for him in Laredo, he'd be able to carry in about five thousand pounds. And that was five thousand dollars. It was the way he'd chosen to make his living, and it was worth it.

The organization was handled by the man in New York, whose name China Blue never said. He was the pilots' agent and he had the connections. He contracted for the jobs, collected the money and sent them the pale green checks that allowed them to live very well.

Outside, the sun had come up to full dawn. It was November and there was a healthy chill in the air. China shivered slightly. He lived on a small ranch in a little town in west Texas. He wouldn't have thought of living anywhere else. He loved this country, loved its green rolling hills, its mesquite and cactus and postoak, loved the land still bedecked with wild flowers even this far into the fall.

Fifty yards behind his house were the horse corrals. As he walked through the grassy dew, one of his quarter horses, the one with the blaze face, came running up to the corral fence, snorting vapor through his nostrils. China walked up to the fence; the horse stuck his head over and he rubbed him between the ears. "You old worthless hide," he said. "I don't know why I don't sell you. You don't do anything except eat and wait for me to bring you a mare. I don't ride you enough to count."

Which was true. Except he liked to sit out in the evenings and look at his horses, admire their symmetry and motion and muscles. He'd never get rid of them. He'd been a rodeo cowboy and the big animals of the Texas country had always been part of his life. He could not imagine not having them around.

Two more of his horses came up and he let them nuzzle him over the fence as he rubbed them behind the ears and gave them an affectionate cussing. After a while he went to the barn, got two buckets of grain and dumped them in the feed trough. The horses came running. He watched them for a moment, then turned and walked toward the little hangar that was at the end of the sod landing strip just behind the horse corral. His personal airplane sat there looking very sleek and very fast. It was a turbo-charged Mooney, to his mind the finest single-engine airplane in the world.

He did a walk-around check, looking it over for any defects, eye-balling the wing tanks for gasoline and looking under the cowling for the oil level. Then he gave it an affectionate pat on the propeller and walked out, leaving the hangar doors open.

When he got back to the house Bonnie was up frying bacon. She looked like such a little girl in the mornings, frowzy and sleepy and very blonde, and always in the same old terry bath robe. She turned her head as he came in and he gave her a light kiss, then went over and sat down at the table. "Where the hell's my breakfast, woman?"

"It's coming, it's coming."

"You better make it damn fast or I'll trade you in on a worthless goat."

From the stove she said, "You don't scare me, boy. You couldn't live without me."

"Try me," he said. "Just try me. It's you who couldn't live without me."

She turned her head then, and smiled at him. "That may be true. You want two eggs or three?"

"Two," he said.

"You want a Coke?"

He made a face. "How many years you been living with me?"

"Only a little over two, even though it feels like a century."

"And how many mornings have I not wanted a Coke?"

"None. But if I didn't ask you, that would be the one morning you'd want coffee."

"Don't even *say* coffee to me. Woman, you are bad. And I don't know why I keep you."

After a few moments she served his eggs and bacon. As she set his plate down, she said, "Are you going to marry me today?"

He shook his head. "No."

"Then are you going to tell me where you got that ridiculous name, China Blue?"

"No."

They had been following this same routine almost every morning since she'd come to live with him after his brother pilot, Terry Alexander, had been killed on that bad run to Mexico.

She sat down across from him with a cup of coffee, watching while he ate. She liked to watch him while he did nearly anything.

He glanced up, feeling her eyes. "You got me packed?"

"Packed? You said you'd only be gone three days at the most. I've put everything you'll need in your little leather bag."

"Did you get my emergency money from the bank?"

"A thousand dollars. It's in your flight kit."

"Okay." He finished eating and leaned back and lit a cigarette.

Bonnie said, "You want anything else to eat?"

He shook his head.

"Then I think I'll brush my hair and put on a face," she said. "You leave with me looking like this, you may not come back."

He watched her go down the hall and a small frown flickered over his face. After Terry died, she'd come to stay a few weeks to get over the grief and shock, but she'd never left. In the time that had passed, she'd come to love him. He thought of her as an amazing woman, strong and pretty and compassionate and very understanding and loving. He loved her, too, but he wasn't going to marry her because of the danger of his work. As he'd told her, "Listen, darlin', you can't ever be a widow again if you don't get married again. So let's just leave things as they are. Okay?"

At first he'd even encouraged her to see other men, but she wouldn't. He encouraged her to make a life of her own, a life independent of him, but she wouldn't. She'd said, "Sorry, I'm a one-man woman and my life is to take care of a man. Hate to tell you this, cowboy, but you're that man. You can wiggle all you want to, but you can't get off the hook."

He had told her then, in fairness, that he wouldn't be tied down. Not to anything or anyone. He'd said, "Look, I might get killed on the next run. Don't count on me for anything. And the only time you can be sure of me is when you see me coming. I'm not promising you anything other than that. You've already been married to one wild flyer, so you know the risks. I want you to stay, but I want you to stay knowing the conditions."

Rather sadly she'd agreed. She'd said, "But do you think you'll ever want to settle down?"

"I don't know," he'd said. "I came into this world an orphan and I expect to go out one. Just don't ever think in terms of me cheating or running around on you, because I don't belong to you or anyone else.''

It had been a brutal scene and he'd hurt her badly. But he'd had no choice. He had been married once, to a woman who'd had a nice blueprint all laid out for his life. When she'd found out that he wasn't about to follow her diagram, the results had been bitter and ugly for both of them.

He didn't intend to make the same mistake twice.

He got up and went back to their bedroom and began to dress. Bonnie had laid out his clothes. He changed his old jeans for a pair in a little better shape, put on a western shirt and then sat down in a chair and pulled on a pair of soft, hand-tooled western boots. After that he slipped into an old leather flying jacket that still had the U.S. Army Air Corps patch on the left shoulder. He'd found it some years back in a clothing store in Mexico, and he'd always wondered how such an article, at least thirty years old at the time he found it, had come to survive in such good shape and end up in a little store in Mexico. He was looking for his hat when the phone rang.

He picked it up and a very familiar voice said, "Let's go rodeoin', cowboy."

It was his best friend, Player, a man he'd known since they'd gone rodeoing when China was sixteen. Many years back, after he'd gotten out of the Air Force, China had taught his friend to fly, and now Player was a venture pilot, too. He said, "I'm not going rodeoing with you. You never pay your half of the gas money and you tell all the girls I'm queer so you can cut me out."

Player said, "Half of that is true."

"How you doing, buddy?"

"Pretty good. Hear you are heading south."

"You been talking to the man."

"Called a little while ago. Looks like I'll be employed in a day or two, depending. Maybe three."

"Any idea what's involved?"

"No. Not at all clear-cut yet. Clients are a little vague."

"Well, watch your ass—considering I'm not there to do it for you."

"Same to you."

He said, "How's your wife and my kids?"

Player chuckled softly. "They're fine. And tell Bonnie I really enjoyed my last visit, the one when you weren't there."

"Why are you calling me up bothering me with your filthy mouth?"

Player laughed again. "Had nothing better to do. And I'm thinking of buying another racehorse and figured you'd want to go in with me again."

China said, "Forget it! I know for a fact you've bought three racehorses and wasn't a one of 'em fast enough to get out of their own way. I wouldn't go with your pick on a horse if you had a race lined up against a turtle."

"That's harsh, buddy. That's harsh. But listen, seriously, why don't you and Bonnie figure to come up here after we both get back. You got a short run and mine ought to be pretty short, too. It sounds pretty routine. Let's all get together and maybe cut a watermelon or something."

China said, "I don't see why not. Maybe you and I could slip off up to Colorado and kill a buck. I'm about ready for some time off."

Player said, "Sounds like a winner."

China was smiling when he hung up. Player always made him smile. He was, to China's mind, the best man he'd ever known, or ever hoped to know. To look at him, Player wasn't very imposing. He was a couple of years older than China and slight and scrawny, with sandy hair and a perpetual cynical grin. He lived, with his wife and two kids, on a ranch similar to China's some three hundred miles northwest. They could not either one of them own a working ranch because they were both gone too much of the time to look after things. But they both had the same consuming need for roots.

"Who was that, baby?" Bonnie called through the half-opened bathroom door.

"That ne'er-do-well, your boyfriend, the ace of the skies."

"Player?"

"None other."

"What did he have to say?"

"Said you were a great lay."

She said, "Tell him thanks."

He pulled a face and went to the bathroom door, just as she began to climb into the tub. "You make another remark like that and we're going to re-enact the shower scene from *Psycho*."

She threw him a wicked grin. "What did he want?"

"For us to come up when we both get back."

"We going?"

"Don't see why not."

He turned away and went back into the kitchen, got another Coke and sat down and lit another cigarette. If anything, Player took more risks than he did as a pilot. It worried him sometimes. From a purely mechanical standpoint, Player was as fine a pilot as he'd ever seen. But he often showed bad judgment in his flying. He'd tried to explain it to his friend once. He'd said, "Pal, you got to quit playing it so close. You're cutting it too fine sometimes."

Player had said, "Thought that was what the job was all about. Hell, *you* take risks."

"I know. But you take gambles."

But Player had been Player ever since he'd known him and he wasn't going to change. Nor was he in a very good position to preach caution to anyone. His whole goddam life had been a risk, beginning with how he'd first managed to luck his way into an orphanage instead of dying God only knew where.

He collected his small traveling bag, instrument case and flight kit. The traveling bag contained just his clothes and shaving gear; in his instrument case were the flying essentials, the maps and charts he would need and the navigational computing equipment. His flight kit was really his survival kit. In it were his .357 magnum revolver, a thousand dollars in cash, a small cache of high protein food, a bottle of halazone tablets for purifying water, a first-aid kit that included penicillin and snakebite antivenom, and a bowie knife.

He took the gear back into the kitchen and set it by the door, then sat down at the table to wait for Bonnie. It was nearly time to leave.

Bonnie came in with her face fixed and her hair brushed; she was wearing a skirt and sweater and looking calendar-girl pretty. "Have I got time to drink a cup of coffee before you leave?" she asked.

"Sure," he said. He lit a cigarette and looked at his watch. It was only a little after eight-thirty. Plenty of time. It was only about a two-hour flight to Laredo. He wanted to be there when they started loading the airplane, and they'd do that sometime after lunch. China Blue insisted on supervising the loading. Once he'd been in a rush and had very carelessly left the job to the ground crew. They'd gotten the center of gravity so far off that the plane had been barely flyable and he'd had his hands full getting it back around the pattern and landing without crashing.

Bonnie got her coffee, stirred in cream and sugar, and then sat there looking pensive. He sighed. She had something on her mind and was about to come out with it. He said, "All right. Go ahead and tell me."

She took a sip and then said, quickly, "You don't want to hear it. You've heard me say it before. You didn't want to hear it then and, anyway, you're not going to listen. So I might as well save my breath."

"Yes," he said, knowing what was coming, "you might as well."

She put her cup down in the saucer. "Well, I'm going to speak my mind again, whether you like it or not."

He drew on his cigarette and waited.

She said, "China, why don't you quit?"

He said, as he'd said before, as he'd said in his marriage, "I don't want to."

"Why not? It's not the money. I handle the money and I know how much you've got. You've got plenty. Plenty for almost anything. You could buy a big ranch and go into that full time. You know you could."

"I don't want to," he said patiently, as if he were speaking to a child. "It's that simple, Bonnie. I don't want to. As Player says, 'It's real simple, cowboy; it ain't complicated.' "

"Why not?"

"Bonnie, look, I'm not a rancher. I'm a flyer. I just keep these few horses and cattle for pets. Or maybe so I can still wear a big hat and boots without feeling like a drugstore cowboy. Who knows the reason? But I'm a flyer. I know you understand that."

She pushed a stray strand of blonde hair back from her face. "But, dammit, there must be some other kind of flying you could do. Why this incessant need to risk your goddam neck!"

"Bonnie, we have been over this. This is the kind of flying I like. I have tried other kinds."

"Well, try them again! God, you could fly for anyone without putting your life on the line every time!"

He said, referring to his ex-wife, knowing the effect it

would have on her, "Bonnie, you are beginning to sound like Madeline."

"Ooooh!" she said, and ran both hands through her hair. "All right, all right, dammit! I'll shut up." She looked down at the table and then smiled quickly at him. "But I feel the need every so often."

He reached over and touched her cheek. She put up both her hands, caught his and pressed it to the side of her head. "China Blue, damn you! You ever going to grow up?"

"If I did, I wouldn't want you. Now let go of me. I got to go."

She stood up as he did and caught him around the waist and hugged. He frowned. He had never been able to convince her that he didn't like long good-byes. He let her cling to him for a moment and then said, gently, "C'mon, baby, I've got to get spurring."

"All right." She released him and then put her face up to be kissed.

He kissed her, not at length and not with passion. She pulled back and looked up at him and shook her head. "Goddammit, just like you were catching the 9:15 commuter train to go in to the office. Shit!"

He laughed. "That's just about what it is. And I'll miss my train if I lallygag with you." He gave her another quick kiss. "See you in a couple of days, baby."

"Will you call me tonight?"

"Maybe," he said.

"Can I come help you roll the plane out?"

"No." He was gathering up his gear at the door. Before going out, he turned back and looked at her. "Listen, go visit someone. Don't hang around here all the time I'm gone."

She shook her head. "No, you might call. You might need me."

He shrugged. "Suit yourself. Bye-bye, baby."

Then he went on out the door and walked through the clear, chilly air toward the hangar. He was frowning as he walked. He wished Bonnie wouldn't be so womanish. Of course, the minute he thought that, it made him smile. He was damn glad she was womanish, or at least feminine, but he guessed what he'd meant was that he wished she wouldn't worry so much. But that was like wishing for the moon; it wasn't going to happen.

At the hangar he opened the door to his plane, stowed his gear on the back seat, found the tow bar, attached it to the nose wheel of the tricycled geared airplane and then pulled it out of the hangar. When it was clear, he disengaged the tow bar, set it inside the hangar and closed the hangar doors.

After that he did another quick walk around and then stepped up on the low wing of the Mooney and slipped inside. Almost immediately he fastened his seat belt and switched on the master. Hearing the battery-driven navigational instruments hum to life, he primed the engine, adjusted the throttle, set the mixture on full, the prop on full for take-off, and then started the engine. It caught instantly, making that full-throated sound he loved so much. He throttled it back, watching the oil gauge for the needles to get into the green. When they were there, he taxied toward the end of his little strip. He'd checked with flight service the night before, so he knew the weather would be clear all the way to Laredo and he'd be flying VFR, Visual Flight Rules.

He paused at the end of his runway to do his run-up check; he ran the engine up to 1500 rpms and then checked the dual magnetos by turning the ignition key first to Left and then to Right. After that he exercised the prop, checked his oil gauge and temperature, checked his gas feed, excercised the elevator and the wing alerieons and the vertical stabilizer, and then pushed the throttle to the wall, trimming the plane as it rushed down the sod field. As the air-speed indicator hit sixty-five, and then seventy knots, he let the plane fly itself off by applying a light touch of back trim. As the plane lifted free, he immediately got the gear up, noted he had two green lights, then lifted the nose slightly and began to climb.

His landing strip was laid out on a heading of one hundred twenty degrees and that was almost the exact heading for Laredo, but instead of continuing straight ahead, he put the plane in a hard bank when he had four hundred feet and came sweeping back toward his house. Beyond the leading edge of the wing he could see Bonnie standing out in the back yard, looking up at him and waving a towel. He grinned and shook his head. She always insisted he make a fly-by before he actually departed. He leveled the plane, waggled his wings in greeting, and then kicked hard right rudder and turned on course for Laredo, climbing as he did.

It was good flying weather, crisp and cloudless. His Mooney, at altitude, would cruise a touch over two hundred knots and he would easily be in Laredo before noon.

He leveled off at 5500 feet, content just to idle along at 2400 rpms. What a life, he thought. What a hell of a life. Looking out the window, he saw the little patches of farms, the roads, the scattered houses, the occasional town, and thought to himself that the people down there didn't quite know what they were missing. Earthbound mortals, he said to himself with good humour. Poor pitiful souls.

Yes, it was a hell of a life. Except for the scattered moments of sheer terror, he was able to live his life the way he wanted to, doing what he loved the best.

He guessed that Bonnie would never really understand the special kind of high he got from his kind of flying— she thought flying was flying—and that was the end of it.

Well, she was wrong there. But she did come as close to understanding it as any woman he'd ever known. God knows, he'd tried all kinds.

Of flying—and women both.

His ticket out of the ordinary had been the Air Force— when he'd been commissioned as a fighter pilot, he'd thought that would be his life forever. But then along had come Viet Nam and he'd resigned his commission. He just couldn't see shooting at people who couldn't shoot back.

He'd been married then, and his wife had been outraged— first, that he would resign from such a promising career, and second, for such an odd reason.

She'd said, "What are you, some sort of cornball idealist? I married you with the expectation you were going to try and make something of yourself—and now this! You don't think they have guns on the other side?"

Patiently he'd tried to explain. "Madeline, you knew when you married me that I don't fight dirty."

"What is *that* supposed to mean?"

"It means I've been a warrior all my life and I never take on anyone who hasn't got a chance against me. It's that simple."

Their marriage hung on through a brief stint with the airlines. He'd done it at his wife's insistence, but a brief taste of the corporate world and orthodox flying techniques had quickly brought out his cynicism. He'd told a friend, "All you get for putting up with their bureaucratic bullshit is a job as an elevator operator. You go up and you go down, all by the numbers."

That was the end of his marriage. After the divorce he drifted around doing odd flying jobs, until he caught on as a corporate pilot flying the president of a small, rich company around in a Lear jet. That had lasted three days; then he found out he was supposed to carry his boss's baggage to the waiting limousine. He'd quit on the spot, saying, "You know, I went all through flight school in the Air Force and I didn't have a single goddamn class in suitcase carrying. I reckon I'm under-qualified for this job."

Then he'd tried crop dusting, which had lasted about as long as any of his other attempts at organized aviation. He'd said, "You seen one row of cotton and you've seen them all. About the only thrill is dodging telephone wires, and I figured I'd better get out of the life as soon as I realized I was getting target fixation on one of Ma Bell's telephone poles."

For a while longer he'd drifted, and occasionally he'd even taken non-flying jobs. Approaching thirty, he'd even considered one more try at rodeoing, but a walk behind the chutes recalled what he'd forgotten—just how big and strong and mean those bulls really were—and he got over that idea in a hurry.

He became a venture pilot by one of those unforseeable strings of coincidence that occasionally come along and change a man's life forever. He'd gotten a freelance job flying some investors into a remote area in southern Mexico. Waiting for them in Mexico City, he'd wandered into the Nicte Ha bar of the Del Prado Hotel and there had run into an old flying buddy from the Air Force named Terry Alexander. Terry had dropped out of the Air Force, too, but he was surprisingly vague about what he was doing. China hadn't been very curious, primarily because he was so preoccupied by his own situation. He was nearly broke and his passengers were already a day late. If they didn't show up, he wasn't sure how he was going to pay his way out of the hotel, much less get back to the States. When Terry sounded him out about how he was doing, China told him baldly that he was just about out of luck. Terry had asked how he felt about becoming a venture pilot and the upshot was a call to the man in New York which got China a new job on a trial basis.

He had loved the life from the very beginning. He'd liked the risk, the adventure, the feeling of a new horizon with each fresh challenge, but, most important, he'd loved the chance to prove himself to his harshest judge, who happened to be himself.

He hadn't stayed on trial very long. Very shortly he had become the ace of the group—the pilot who would take jobs other pilots turned down, the pilot who nearly always found a way to bring off a seemingly impossible assignment. It was very seldom that a complaint ever reached the man in New York about China.

Now, with nothing but blue sky all around him, he tuned the VOR receiver on the instrument panel to the frequency of the ohmni transmitter at the Laredo airport. He made a slight course correction; the needle centered and then he was on a dead heading for his destination. After that there wasn't much to do except tune the VHF radio to a country-western station, flick on the automatic pilot, light a cigarette and sit back and enjoy the view.

He remembered Player's phone call and grinned to himself. That was a good idea, for them to get together when they both got off assignment. They could both probably use a little rest. He and Bonnie would go on up to Player's ranch, and he and his old partner could get a little drunk together, tell a few lies, raise a little hell. Only thing was, they couldn't go off and chase ass the way they used to, for Player took his marriage pretty seriously and had just flat quit fooling around. That had surprised him, Player getting married. He hadn't counseled against it, obviously, as it was Player's life and Player would have just told him to go to hell even if he had said something. But he didn't really think that he or Player or any other man in their line of work ought to get married. And not just because it was hard on the woman—it was that, too—but because of what it did to the man. Those kinds of ties gave a man too much to be afraid to lose. And when a man had something he was afraid to lose, it weakened him, made him too cautious, took the steel of decision out of him. In their line of work a man very often had no time to hang back and consider a decision; he had to act with instant reflexes. And if a man was thinking too much about his wife and home and kids, it could make him that fatal hair-second too slow. A man doing what they were doing, he'd often thought to himself, shouldn't let anyone get too close to him and he shouldn't get too close to them.

But then, he'd never been much one for letting too much closeness into his life anyway.

Just then he glanced at his watch and noted that he should be coming in range of Laredo. He set the UHF radio to the Laredo frequency, then thumbed the mike and said, "Laredo approach control, this is Mooney two-two-four-four tango heading one-two-five degrees inbound for a landing. Estimate forty miles northwest, altitude five-five-zero-zero, squawking one-two-zero-zero. Go ahead."

In a moment the voice of the approach controller came back: "Mooney two-two-four-four tango, Laredo approach, ident and continue inbound."

He complied by punching the ident button on the transponder so that his aircraft would appear as a blip on the radar controller's screen. Then he throttled back to 2000 rpms and began his descent.

He began singing a little country-western ballad as he readied the airplane for his arrival. "*As I walked out in the streets of Laredo, as I walked out in Laredo one day. . . . I spied a young cowboy all wrapped in white linen, wrapped in white linen as cold as the clay . . .*"

Damn, he thought, if I could sing I'd be dangerous.

Chapter Two

After he'd landed and seen to his airplane, he took a taxi
and went straight to the offices of Avila Gomez, the man
he'd be flying the load in for. Gomez owned a freight
forwarding company and China assumed that he sometimes acted as a legitimate transfer agent for goods bound
into Mexico, but he figured Gomez's main income came
from smuggling in electronic and other high import
commodities.

His offices were down near the train terminal, near the
International Bridge, and it was a long, bumpy ride over
the unpaved back streets of the Mexican border town. At
the warehouse where Gomez had his headquarters China
got out and paid the driver, then went up the dusty walk to
the little office at the corner of the building. Even though
it was fall everywhere else, it was still hot in Laredo.
Fortunately, he had taken off his leather coat and left it in
the airplane. He entered a shabby, little outer office with a

male clerk sitting at a desk. The door to Gomez's office was open and China pointed. "He in there?"

"Yes," the man said. "Walk right on in,"

"Thanks." China gave the door frame a couple of bangs with his fist and then went on in. Gomez was sitting behind his desk with his tie undone, smoking a cigar and sweating his shirt through.

"Hello, amigo" he said, looking up. "Hot, no?"

China slumped into a chair. "Gomez, you cheap bastard, as much money as you make, why the hell don't you buy an air conditioner for this damn office?"

Gomez shrugged. "It's not always this hot."

"Bullshit," China said. "I've never been down here when it wasn't hot."

Gomez shrugged again and yawned. He was a fat Mexican-American who spoke with only a trace of an accent. His shirt sleeves were rolled up to show heavy, hairy forearms. "Maybe one day I'll think to get one. It isn't a question of money."

"Bullshit," China repeated. He got out a cigarette and lit it. "It's always a question of money with you. Now what have you got for me to fly?"

Gomez waved his cigar in a congratulatory manner, "Why, the super bird! As always."

China regarded him sourly. The super bird Gomez was talking about was a tired old DC-3 that barely stayed within the legal FAA standards. China said, "Gomez, have you had the maintenance done on that thing since I was here last? The maintenance I insisted you have done before I flew it again?"

Gomez waved his cigar again. "The airplane is in tip-top condition. I give you my word on this. My personal guarantee."

"Hah!" China said. He glanced over in the corner at an

old refrigerator that was making a humming noise. "You got any beer in that thing? Or anything cold to drink?"

"But of course," Gomez said. "Allow me, amigo." He got up and, moving surprisingly fast for a man of his size, opened the door, took out a cold can and handed it to China. For himself he took a diet soft drink. He patted himself on the belly. "Maybe need to lose a pound or two."

China sipped reflectively on his beer, letting the coolness run down his throat and soothe his stomach. He didn't really expect the DC-3 to be in any better shape, hadn't expected it to be when he took the job. Gomez wasn't going to spend a nickel more than he had to. But that didn't matter. China knew he could get the old bird up and down with probably no trouble. That was the beauty of the old DC-3's; they kept flying even when they weren't supposed to. China said, "Well, where to this time?"

Gomez got up. To one side of the refrigerator a big map of Mexico was pinned to the sparse wall. China got up and followed the Mexican to the map. Gomez took a pencil and made a little mark on the map. "Here," he said. "Here is an old deserted strip we have never used before. It will be very safe."

China studied the mark. It was about a hundred and fifty miles southwest from Laredo. The nearest big town was Monclova, about fifteen miles to the east. The map was not a terrain map, but China knew that that part of Mexico was rough country. He said, "How come this strip? Whose was it?"

Gomez flicked ashes from his cigar on the floor and then stuffed the stub in his mouth. "An old landing strip that a mining company used to use. They are out of business. But the strip is in very good shape. Very smooth and very easy to find."

China glanced at him. "Oh yeah? How do you know?"

"I have a man there in Monclova. That is how the strip came to my attention. As you know I am always on the lookout for new landing strips so that we will stay ahead of the *policia*. For the safety of my pilots."

China grunted, not bothering to reply. He continued to study the map, noting that he'd be heading right into the Sierra Madres, or at least into their foothills. Probably the strip lay in a little valley. He had a topographical chart of the area back in his map case at the plane and would be able to tell more then. He said, "And you claim your man has looked this strip over?"

Gomez took a handkerchief out of his pocket and wiped at the sweat on his face. "*Certamente*. Yes, indeed."

"Recently?"

"Very recently."

"I bet the goddam thing's three foot high in weeds and indistinguishable from the surrounding country."

"Oh no, no, no" Gomez said. "It's in first-class condition. I give you my personal guarantee."

China said, "I wish to hell you'd quit giving me your personal guarantee. I know about what that's worth." He went back to his chair and sat down. He knew the strip would be a mess—and hell to find on top of it. But that was part of the job; that was why he got paid such good money, too.

Gomez went back to his desk, mopping at his neck with the handkerchief. He said, "No, I assure you about this landing strip. It was the perfection of it, both in its condition and its remoteness that caused me to call our mutual friend in New York. Don't forget, amigo, it is I who would have a great deal of money to lose if the airplane had trouble landing or if there were problems with the police."

China got up. "You have my sympathy, Gomez. All I

have to lose is my ass. You got the crew lined up to load that son-of-a-bitch early this afternoon?''

"Oh yes. They will be there at two. You have time for a good lunch. Will you eat with me?''

"No,'' China said shortly. He didn't eat with people he didn't like. He said, "I'm going to go back to the airport, get my gear, and check into a motel and get cleaned up. Your people better be there at two. I don't want to wait around that airport all afternoon.''

"Do you know the exact hour you will be leaving in the morning? I have to get word to my man in Monclova so he can have the trucks there to meet you. It wouldn't do for them to be hanging around too long.''

China said, "I thought you told me this airstrip was really remote.''

"Oh, it is,'' Gomez said. "Still, it's better not to take chances.''

"I can't say for sure until I check the weather. But I don't think it's going to change. I think you can figure I'll get off at about six a.m., and it shouldn't be more than an hour and fifteen minutes flying time to the rendezvous with your trucks. I'll call you tonight and say for sure.'' He started for the door and paused. "How much am I carrying.''

Gomez shrugged. "About six thousand pounds.''

"Not *about*, Gomez. Exactly.''

"All right, all right.'' Gomez pulled open a drawer and took out some papers. He looked at them for a moment and then said, "Five thousand, eight hundred and sixty-eight. Pounds.''

"And every crate and every carton is individually weight-marked?''

"Of course,'' Gomez said. "I understand that. It's important for the correct loading of the airplane. You tell me that every time. Don't you think I understand it is necessary by now?''

"Sure," China said. "And every time there are plenty that aren't marked."

Gomez shrugged. "Some of my men make mistakes."

China said, "Have your man out here drive me out to the airport. I'll call you tonight."

China rode back to the airport in Gomez's pickup with the warm wind blowing through the open window. Laredo was not a very pretty town, but then most border towns weren't. They were too full of poverty, too full of corruption, too full of a populace that couldn't decide if it was Anglo or Mexican.

At the airport he collected his gear and then had one of the flight line attendants drive him to a nearby motel. They all knew him and why he was in town. But, of course, it wasn't illegal to load a plane with electronic gear on the U.S. side. It was just illegal to fly it to Mexico without notifying the Mexican authorities.

The attendant was a young kid that China knew spent most of his salary on flight lessons. He was in awe of a pilot like China. He said, "Going to make another run, China?"

"Something like that."

The kid was chewing gum and he shifted it around for a moment. Then he asked, "Don't reckon there'd ever be a chance for me to go along, would there?"

China shook his head. "Think not, Kenny. It is Kenny, isn't it?"

"Yessir."

"How many hours you got now, Kenny?"

"Nearly thirty. I take my written test next week. Boy, that's what's got me worried."

"Well, study hard. Stay after the books. That's the only way to pass that written."

"When you loading out?"

"This afternoon."

"Would, ah, would you mind if I come watch? I hear there's a lot of weight and balance problems on that written test and I might learn something watching you."

China smiled slightly, thinking back to his cadet days. "No, come ahead," he said, "though I don't think you'll learn much. Nowadays I don't exactly go by the book."

"That don't matter," the kid said. "It'd still be a real privilege for me—watching a pilot like you in operation."

At the motel China thanked the kid, refused his offer to carry his bags, and went in and registered. When he got to his room, the air conditioning was a great relief from the dusty heat outside. He dumped his bags on the bed, stripped off his clothes and took a quick shower. Toweling off, he began to feel better. He hadn't taken the time to shave that morning before leaving, so now he got out his shaving kit and stood naked in front of the big mirror and lathered up. As he shaved, he reviewed the upcoming run in his mind, probing for eventualities and possibilities and danger factors. The two main danger factors were the condition of the airplane he'd be flying and the possible presence of the Mexican police at the other end. The plane didn't worry him. In fact, he'd flown DC-3's in worse shape than Gomez's dilapidated old bird. The police—well, that was something he had to take on trust, trust that Gomez had picked the right spot to land the goods, trust that there hadn't been a leak, trust that some freak coincidence wouldn't put the police in the area just as he landed. That was all part of the job.

In the mirror he looked at his bare chest and half-congratulated himself on how few scars it bore. There was the little scar under his left collarbone where a small bore bullet had entered and then gone cleanly out the back. That had come from a lady client who'd thought she was going to hijack him and his airplane and be flown to Haiti. The embarrassing thing about it was that she'd managed to shoot him with her little .22 purse gun before he could wrestle it away from her.

Then there was a jagged slash of scar tissue across his chest, a souvenir from a crash landing in a Cessna 182 in the Peruvian Andes. The only other scar from flying was a bullet wound in his foot. Actually it wasn't a bullet wound; it was shrapnel from the right rudder pedal. He'd been picking up some political refugees off a beach in Columbia and the bad guys had come bursting out of the jungle just as he was gaining altitude after taking off. They'd opened fire with automatic weapons and one of the bullets had come through the bottom of the plane and—struck the right rudder pedal. The impact of the bullet had torn off a piece of the rudder pedal and it had ripped through China's foot. But that was a scar he was grateful for, because if the bullet hadn't hit the pedal its trajectory would have carried it right on into his upper body. As it was, his passenger in the copilot's seat had been killed, and another one in the back seat had been wounded so badly that he'd nearly bled to death before China could get them safely to Caracas and get medical help.

But it wasn't too bad a score, not for as long as he'd been flying. Hell, he thought, looking at himself, I been hurt plenty worse rodeoing.

Which was true. He'd had his neck broken, when a bull had turned over in the chute with him; his leg broken; both collarbones broken; a punctured lung from a broken rib; and his nose and fingers broken more times than he could count.

And hadn't made anywhere near as much money as he did flying.

"That's what it's all about," he said aloud, cheerfully. "You got to get the most money you can when you're trading off pieces of yourself. There's only so much to sell."

He put shaving lotion on his face and then dressed, putting on a clean pair of jeans and a fresh shirt that Bonnie had packed for him. After that he went to the motel restaurant, which was as good as any, and ate enchiladas and tacos and guacamole salad and drank a couple of cold beers. The flight line boy, Kenny, had offered to come back and get him, but he took a cab for the short ride out to the airport.

He had the driver pull up in front of the hangar that Gomez leased. He paid the cab off and then walked through the heat to a little side door and stepped into the cool dimness of the hangar. The big doors were closed at each end of the hangar—for secrecy, he supposed. Which was a laugh, since everyone on the airfield knew Gomez was ready to send another load to his brother-in-law, the appliance king, in Mexico.

The DC-3 was parked in the middle of the hangar, its side cargo door open. Two trucks were pulled alongside it and several workers were standing around, obviously waiting for him. He could see that they'd placed a ramp up to the open cargo door.

He walked up to the little group. Gomez's clerk, the one who'd driven China to the motel, was standing there, a clipboard in his hand. "Hello, Pepe," China said. The clerk handed him the clipboard. China took a moment to run his eyes over the list of weights. Then he took out a flight computer and figured out his center of gravity. When he was through, he nodded to the clerk. "Let's get it loaded."

He stood there, checking off items as the men went up the cargo ramp with the cartons. As he checked off each box, he'd tell the handler "forward" or "amidships" or "aft".

It took about two hours to load the plane. When the men were finished, he went aboard and made sure all the boxes and cartons were securely lashed. He'd had a load get loose on him in the middle of turbulent air once, and that was an experience he never wanted to repeat.

When he was satisfied that the plane was correctly loaded, he came through the door, shut it and locked it behind him. He said to the clerk, "Pepe, I don't want anybody near this airplane the rest of the night. *Comprende?*"

"For sure, Señor Blue," Pepe said. "I personally am to stay this night with the plane. My wife is to bring my supper to me here."

"That's fine," China said. "Just be goddam sure nobody goes near it. I got it just like I want it."

"Señor Gomez has ordered me to stay. So you see all will be in order."

China handed him the clipboard. "Well, you do what good old Señor Gomez tells you to do."

Pepe said, "Further, señor, I am to go with you tomorrow."

China was a little surprised. "The hell you say! What's the matter, doesn't he trust his brother-in-law to give him a straight count at the other end?"

Pepe just smiled and shrugged. "That is a thing I don't know, señor."

China smiled. "I bet that's it. I bet one of the appliance kings doesn't trust the other. Are you supposed to check them off to the man at the other end?"

"That is what I am to do, Señor."

China said, "Well, I don't give a damn. Just don't get airsick."

The clerk didn't say anything. China thought he looked a little worried. He said, "You have flown before, haven't you?"

Pepe gave his head a quick shake. "No, señor. Never."

China shrugged. "Well, good luck. Hope they don't shoot at us."

He left the clerk looking considerably worried. But, thought China, if I've got to be scared, he might as well be scared too.

The line boy, Kenny, came running up as China stepped out of the hangar. He hadn't been able to get away from his job, he said, to watch China loading the plane.

"You didn't miss anything, son. It's just all part of being careful. The how of being careful ain't important; the thinking careful is what counts."

He hooked a ride back to his motel with the boy. It was not quite six o'clock, still too early to eat, so he went to his room and rested for a couple of hours. He thought of calling Bonnie, but decided he'd do it later. Then he grinned when he thought of how he'd pontificated to the young boy about being careful. He said to himself, I sure wish you'd practice what you preach, ace. We might live longer.

He got up in the late evening, dressed, and took a cab to the International Bridge and then walked across to Mexico. As always, he was struck by two things: the poverty and the amazing number of police, both local and the *Federales*. They were all over, slouching about in their khaki uniforms, carrying guns, and looking official. Walking down the broken sidewalk, seeing the dilapidated cars in the streets, the shabby shops, the endless string of beggars, he always wondered what they needed so many police for. God knew, there didn't seem to be much worth stealing.

And he'd heard of Mexican prisons. He knew of a couple of American smugglers who'd been put in Mexican jails, and their advice was to stay the hell out of them.

Well, he never intended to see the inside of any jail, Mexican or otherwise.

He walked to the Cadillac Bar and Grill, an old establishment in Nuevo Laredo, ate a steak and some fruit, and then sat watching the people passing up and down the street from his table by the window. Because of his early morning flight, he limited himself to two beers and no hard liquor. He sat there smoking, not thinking about much except getting the run over with and getting back home and taking a little time off. Truth be told, he was a little tired. He mentally counted up. Over the last two months he'd made nine runs, which was quite a lot. Some of them had been as simple as carrying golf clubs into Canada to beat the duty, but one flight in particular had been a little hairy. He'd been hired as a bonded courier to transport a half-million dollars worth of diamonds from the East coast to the West coast, a service he'd performed many times before. Usually it was a milk run, but this time the airplane he'd been flying, a twin-engine Piper Navajo, had developed a total electrical failure midway through the flight. It had been night, dark as pitch, and he'd had to use a flashlight to see what few instruments, those that ran off a vacuum, he had left. Then the starboard engine had gone out and he'd had to make a forced landing in the middle of the Arizona desert. He'd managed somehow, to get the airplane down without serious damage, but because of the electrical failure, he hadn't been able to report trouble and give his position, so it had been an uncomfortable three-day wait before search planes had finally located him.

It had not been a pleasant time. The first day he'd run out of food, the second out of water, and the third out of cigarettes—all that in the middle of a desert in early September when it was almost too hot to breathe. When they'd finally got him back to civilization, he'd lost ten pounds.

And on top of everything else, Bonnie had been beside herself with worry, convinced after so much time had passed with no word that he was dead. That had created a bad scene and provoked her to begin anew her campaign to make him quit the venture organization.

A pretty girl walked by outside the window and smiled at China. He smiled back and watched her progress down the sidewalk, admiring her ass and the back of her legs. But she was probably a *puta*, a whore, he thought. Nice girls in Mexico, no matter how pretty, didn't smile at strange men in cafes.

Sure enough, after a few moments she passed by again, this time going the other way. She smiled even bigger at China and seemed about to pause. Yes, he thought, she's a whore. He called for his check and started back to the American side and to his hotel. He didn't mind a woman being a whore; everybody had to make their living the best they could. But he was damned if *he* was going to pay for it. He'd been with a few whores in his time, but it had always been dutch treat; he didn't charge them and they didn't charge him.

After he got in bed he called Bonnie.

She said, "Hi, baby, how you doing?"

"Just guessing and gambling, as always. Just thought I'd call to say good night."

They talked a few moments more and then he said good-bye. She said, "I love you, China."

He said, "I love you, girl. Good night."

Chapter Three

He got off just before dawn, lumbering the overloaded old plane down the runway and using up a good bit of it before finally becoming airborne. But once clear of the ground and wheels up the plane flew well enough.

Needless to say, he had not filed a flight plan. Only a very few were supposed to know he was about to violate Mexican airspace without a clearance.

He set a heading a little to the southwest, then flicked on the automatic pilot and lit a cigarette. He had Pepe strapped into a bucket seat in the back. He didn't particularly like first-time flyers sitting in the copilot's seat, especially when some fine-honed flying might be called for. They tended to get in the way at the wrong time.

After he'd leveled the airplane off at five thousand feet, he unstrapped his safety harness and went into the rear compartment. Pepe was sitting in the little bucket seat with his hands clenched in his lap and his eyes squinted shut.

China laughed. "Hey, old buddy, it's all right. *Muy seguridad.*"

Pepe opened his eyes and then opened them even wider as he looked at China. "But, señor, who is driving the airplane?"

He tried to explain about the automatic pilot, then gave up and went forward, got a bottle of cognac out of his flight kit, and brought it back and handed it to the Mexican. "Have a pull on this," he said.

The little Mexican took it gratefully and helped himself to one long drink, and then another. China hastily retrieved the bottle and corked it. "Hell," he said, "I just want you to loosen up a little, not get so relaxed you can't move."

After Pepe had calmed down, China went back to the cockpit and settled in behind the wheel. From his map case he took out a chart for northern Mexico. The problem with this flight, as with all such flights, was that he couldn't use electronic navigation aids, but had to rely on dead reckoning to get him to the approximate area and then on visual contact to locate his exact target. Studying the chart, he finally found the little airfield. It was marked with an X across it to show it was no longer in use. As he'd guessed, it was in a little valley surrounded by mountains, but none of them were over 4500 feet above sea level. He picked out the most prominent of peaks surrounding the abandoned airstrip and set a course for it. The only other ground check he'd have would be a *chiquita puebla*, a tiny village, some two miles south of the strip. If he saw that, he'd know he'd over flown his target.

He glanced at his watch. They'd been flying about forty five minutes and, at calculated ground speed of one hundred fifty knots, he figured they ought to be getting close. He peered ahead, trying to pick out the peak he was aiming for. It was a good day for flying, clear and bright, but with a high layer of cirrus clouds that blocked off the sun's glare.

Then he spotted his mountain, made a slight course correction to the right, pulled power and began his descent to look the area over.

He held the peak just slightly to his right as he descended, lower and lower, until he was below the apex of the little row of mountains and the valley was opening up before him. There was a brown sameness to the terrain that made it hard to pick out any distinguishing features. At five hundred feet above the ground he leveled off and made a sweeping pass up the valley, which was three or four miles across, without seeing anything that looked remotely like an airstrip, abandoned or not.

At the end of the valley he climbed to avoid the mountains, made a left turn, descended and began a search a mile further over.

Then, about halfway down the valley on the pass, he spotted an oblong stretch of ground where the underbrush and the grass were shorter than the surrounding countryside. It was obviously the strip he was looking for. He descended to a hundred feet above ground, throttled back even more, and slowly flew the airplane down the stretch while he inspected the ground he was going to land on. Just then he caught a flash of light off to his right. Looking quickly, he glimpsed the outline of three trucks pulled up near the strip, but almost hidden by the underbrush.

At the end of his survey he pulled up and made another pass, looking the terrain over and noting the direction of the wind. At the end of the valley he made another turn back, this time flying directly over the trucks. He could distinctly see them now, and he wondered idly why there were three of them when there had only been two back in Laredo. But then, what the hell did he know about trucks? Nothing, and less about Mexican trucks. Maybe they couldn't haul as much as Texas trucks, or maybe they weren't the same size. Beside the trucks he could see several figures, all staring at him with up-turned faces.

Well, as near as he could figure, he could set the plane down on the strip and maybe have a chance of not getting killed. The grass was pretty high, but a DC-3 was meant to land in high grass, and he hadn't seen any serious-sized rocks or any holes larger than average in the ground. He stuck his head around the companionway door and yelled for Pepe to check his seat belt. Then he pulled his own seat belt tighter and put down the landing gear.

He was taking a long, low approach. He wanted the airplane to be flying just as slowly as it would when he touched down. The gear was down and the green lights on the instrument panel indicated it was locked into position. Watching his air speed he slowly cranked in thirty degrees of flaps. His speed dropped to seventy knots and he cranked in another fifteen degrees, holding the nose slightly down. The end of the strip, or what he took to be the end of the strip, was coming up rapidly. He pulled off most of the power, felt the bird sink, and then jockeyed the wheel back and forth, holding it right on the thin edge of stalling. Then the ground was there and he felt the wheels whispering through the high grass and he was touching down and rolling. He kept the power on, but gradually pulled back on the wheel to let the tail wheel settle slowly on the ground. It was bumpy, but he hadn't blown a tire or ruined the hydraulics in the landing gear.

He cut power further, then slowly taxied toward the end of the strip where he'd seen the trucks. As he got abreast of them, he kicked in the right rudder and wheeled the plane around so that it was pointing back up the strip.

He did not shut off his engines, just left them ticking slowly over. He was going to keep them running until they got the plane unloaded, and then he was going to pour on the power and get the hell out of Mexico and go home and see Bonnie—and relax. Strangely, thinking about it, he suddenly missed her, a thing he'd been finding himself doing more and more often of late—a thing he'd have to fight against.

He stuck his head around the companionway door and yelled for Pepe to get the cargo door opened and to get the airplane unloaded. "And make it damn quick! I want to get out of here."

He was parked very near the side of the strip and the weeds on that side were taller than a man's head. He kept watching, waiting for the trucks to emerge and come up to the airplane. Behind him he heard Pepe opening the cargo door.

Then, out of the corner of his eye, he saw movement to his right and to the front of the airplane. Khaki-uniformed policemen, *Federales,* were rushing from the tall grass, their rifles at the ready, and running toward the airplane.

"Oh shit!" he said. Without hesitation he released the emergency brake and slammed both throttles forward. The big engines roared and, slowly, the airplane began to move. In front of him a few of the policemen were waving their arms and motioning for him to stop. As he picked up speed and began to bear down on them, he saw them raise their rifles. He ducked as low as he could in the seat.

Now the plane was moving with speed and the police were falling behind. Dimly, over the roar of the engines, he heard the crack of the rifles. Glass shattered in his windscreen as a bullet came through the window on the passenger's side and exited through the front. He could hear, almost feel, bullets smacking into the skin of the airplane. Out the side window he saw a sudden line of holes appear in the wing. They had automatic weapons.

"Move, move, move!" he said aloud, trying to will the

airplane to get flying speed, to get off the ground, to get out of range of the guns.

If they caught him, it would mean a Mexican prison for sure. And oh God, he wouldn't be able to take that. Not penned up, not without Bonnie, not able to be free.

And then the tail was coming up and the wheel began to feel lighter and more responsive in his hand. He cranked in fifteen degrees of flap, then another fifteen. His air-speed indicator read eighty knots, normally fast enough for liftoff, but not fast enough for the load he was carrying this time.

It seemed he could still hear the bullets smacking into the plane. Out the window he could see where a line of fire had stitched the left wing. It had hit the wing tank on that side and streams of gas were spraying back and vaporizing in the air.

But he wasn't worrying about fuel; he had plenty to get out of the valley, and that was all he wanted.

"C'mon plane, c'mon!" he said.

Finally he felt the wheels lift clear and he was flying. He got the gear up as quickly as he could, then felt the plane lift a little as it lost that drag. Ahead was a low mountain ridge, rising in front of him a mile or so off. It seemed to get higher as he struggled for altitude.

He glanced at his altimeter. He was maybe two hundred feet above the ground. Then he felt rather than heard the starboard engine skip a beat.

He glanced across the cockpit and out the passenger window. He couldn't see if it had been hit.

Then it missed again. He felt his heart in his throat and a sick feeling in the pit of his stomach.

Not now, he thought. Oh, please, not now.

Ahead the ridge was coming closer and he needed at least another two hundred feet of altitude.

Then the engine began to stutter in earnest, firing and

missing and then catching and roaring for a second and then missing again.

He felt the airplane falter slightly and he depressed the nose to try to gain more flying speed.

He glanced again at the engine, but was unable to see where it had been hit. It couldn't be fuel. And it couldn't be carburetion.

It was that goddam magneto he'd told Gomez to have fixed.

"That goddam son-of-a-bitch!" he said aloud. "I'll kill that bastard."

The engine was missing badly now and he put out his hand to kill it and feather the prop. Then he withdrew it. The DC-3 would fly on one engine, but not when it was so heavily loaded. If he lost the engine, he wasn't going to make it over the ridge.

To the left and to the right of the ridge the mountains rose higher. And if he made a 180-degree turn, he would fly right back over the police.

He babied the airplane, coaxing every foot of altitude out of it he could. When he felt he had enough air speed to handle it, he cranked in the last fifteen degrees of flaps. The plane slowed, right on the thin edge of stalling, but it lifted a few feet higher.

The engine was still misfiring, only occasionally surging at full power. Ahead, the ridge was coming up, still above him. He stared at it, quite calmly wondering if he were fixing to crash, maybe to get killed.

He tried a gentle turn to the right and then a similar turn back to the left, flying S-turns, hoping to delay the ridge's rush to meet him, hoping to gain flying space to gain altitude.

He babied the yoke, holding the airplane right on the verge of stall, fighting for every foot of altitude he could get.

And then the engine suddenly backfired and missed—for a heart-stopping second went silent. Even with the roar of the port engine there suddenly came a quiet so loud China could almost hear it.

With the loss of the engine the airplane began to shudder, began to stall. China depressed the nose, trying to keep it flying.

The ridge was just there, only about a quarter of a mile ahead, rushing toward him with sickening speed. And still above him.

And then the engine suddenly came back to life, roaring with a full throttle surge. China felt the airplane lift and begin climbing.

The ridge was so close now that China could see the individual features of it, rocky and hard and jagged.

With both engines roaring he depressed the nose, saw the air-speed indicator shoot up, and then, just before the crash could come, he suddenly pulled back on the yoke and the airplane climbed and lifted and the ridge skimmed slowly by below him.

He let go the wheel with his right hand and tried to wipe some of the perspiration off his brow, but the palm of his hand was too wet to do any good. The perspiration was down in his eyelashes and stinging his eyes. He jerked up his shirt and rubbed quickly at them.

"Oh shit!" he said, and let out a long sigh.

He suddenly thought of the little Mexican clerk. He put his head around the door and yelled back, "Pepe! Pepe!"

There was no answer. He yelled again.

Listening, he heard a roar from the rear of the plane and he remembered that Pepe had already opened the cargo door when the *Federales* descended on them. He'd never gotten a chance to close it as quickly as China had taken off.

God, China thought, how did this damn plane manage to stay in the air?

Well, he felt bad about Pepe. If the police had got him, he'd be going to jail, but if he'd been in the cargo hold, with all the bullets that were coming through he'd probably be dead. China hoped for the little Mexican's sake that he'd stayed in the cargo hold.

He wanted to go see, but as delicate as the flying was, he dared not leave the controls for a second.

He nursed the plane up, fought for more altitude. He didn't know if there were official Mexican planes searching for him or not. All he knew was that he was a hundred and fifty miles from the U.S. border with a sick bird and he wanted to get as high as he could.

At three thousand feet the starboard engine quit with a finality that told him it wasn't going to restart. He quickly feathered the prop and settled down to the grim business of keeping the plane aloft as long as he could. He knew he'd never reach the border; as overloaded as he was, he was on nothing but a long glide. He was going to stretch it as far as he could. Perhaps he could get close enough to the border to cross it overland.

He thought of going back and trying to jettison some of the cargo, but he knew that he'd never be able singlehandedly to push the cargo door back against the rush of the wind. And even if he could, the sudden drag might overbalance the automatic pilot and he didn't have enough altitude to give him time to scramble back to the cockpit before the airplane would likely crash.

But he could risk going back to shut and secure the door. At least he could eliminate that drag. He cautiously set the automatic pilot, waited a few moments to see how the plane was going to act, then quickly undid his safety harness, jumped out of his seat and ran back to the cargo cabin.

It was a mess. Just at a quick glance he could tell that over a hundred bullets had come through the fuselage. The cartons were shot up and splintered and there was glass and pieces of TVs and stereos scattered all over the floor.

There was no sign of Pepe.

The cargo door was slightly ajar, held in place by the force of the wind. He took the big handle, tugged it shut, then locked it. He felt the airplane adjust slightly as the drag was reduced. Fearful this far from the controls, he quickly scrambled back up the aisle and into his cockpit seat. He glanced at the altimeter. He was down to 2500 feet.

He flew on. The mountains were behind him, but the country was still rough—hilly and rocky, and filled with cactus and stunted trees. A landing on such terrain, even wheels-up, would be nothing but a controlled crash.

Occasionally he would spot a little patch of level ground and be slightly tempted to go ahead and land while he still had some control of the airplane and altitude to work with. But then, looking down at the bleak, lonesome-looking country, he would dismiss the idea and just hope he could stretch the powered glide as far as possible.

He had the port engine firewalled and running on full power and full rich mixture. Sooner or later that kind of flying would burn the engine up, but he didn't reckon there was going to be much left of the airplane anyway, not at the rate things had been going.

His air-speed indicator was sitting on seventy five knots. Occasionally he would gently try to lift the nose, hoping to gain at least a few feet of altitude, but each time he tried, the airplane would begin to shudder as it approached stall and he would have to let the nose back down.

The altimeter was unwinding slowly, falling to 2000 feet and then 1700 and then 1500. He glanced at his watch. As near as he could figure, he'd been in the air about half an hour. But at his current speed he doubted he'd come more than fifty miles.

It was still a long way to the border.

At 1200 feet he knew he was running out of time. He began studying the terrain, peering far ahead, looking for some place to set the bird down. The country was amazingly empty. Twice since he'd left the little valley, he'd seen tiny villages, settlements of a few mud-walled huts with thatched roofs. And occasionally he'd seen an isolated little rancho with a shack and a few rundown corrals surrounding it. But mostly the country seemed uninhabited.

At one thousand feet he began looking in earnest, resolved now to take the next likely looking place he saw.

But, if anything, it seemed as if the country had gotten rougher. Ahead it even appeared as if a low line of hills was coming up.

At eight hundred feet he saw a little green patch ahead, but he was too far away to tell how big it was. If it was green, he thought, it had to be near some sort of civilization. Everything else was brown.

He coaxed the airplane, trying to prevent the altimeter needle from unwinding at such an alarming rate. Sweat was starting out on his forehead. Everything below him looked rocky and jagged enough to tear the bottom right out of the plane.

The green patch grew bigger the nearer he got.

At seven hundred feet he could tell it was some sort of meadow, with either cows or sheep grazing in it. At the upper end something taller than grass seemed to be growing.

He banked slightly to the right, so as to keep the patch to his left where he could get a clear view.

Then, back from the field about a quarter of a mile and to his right, he saw a little house up on a hill. It was whitewashed and in much better shape than anything he'd seen in the vast wasteland that surrounded it.

But he couldn't take the time to more than glance at it. He was flying along beside the field now and he could see it had looked deceptively smooth from a distance. There were plenty of rocks in it and a good share of the little stunted trees that seemed to grow so well in that part of Mexico. He looked at the corn field, judged it to be a good five or six hundred feet long. His best plan, he immediately saw, was to try and land at the end of the corn field, plow through it, and hope the airplane had slowed enough before he hit the rocks and trees in the pasture.

But it really didn't matter; he was fixing to land somewhere, whether he wanted to or not. He turned slightly to the right, the plane dropping lower as he banked. Then he made a long sweeping turn back to the left and lined up on the corn field.

His altimeter showed three hundred feet above the ground.

He was committed now. For a second he thought he was going to be short of the corn field and he immediately put in fifteen degrees of flap. The plane lifted slightly and he saw he was going to be all right.

He intended to make a full stall landing. He was going to cut all power a quarter of a mile from the end of the strip, have it flying as slowly as he could, and then pull it up into a full stall just before touchdown.

It was still going to be rough, no matter how much he managed to brake the plane.

Once he hit the ground, he'd just be a passenger, with no control over the airplane whatsoever.

At a distance he judged to be proper he pulled power on the port engine, feathered it, and then cranked in fifteen degrees more of flap. With the last engine out there came a sudden quiet. He could hear the wind whistling through the bullet hole in the windscreen.

Out his window he noted that the punctured gas tank on the left wing was still leaking gas. Well, there was nothing he could do about that. There was no way to jettison gas on a DC-3. All he could hope for was not to make any sparks in the wrong places.

Just before touchdown he turned off the master switch, killing all electrical power. The corn field was rushing toward him, so close now that he could see the tassels on the top of the stalks. Then he could feel them brushing against the belly of the plane.

At the last instant he pulled the nose of the airplane up; it stalled with a shudder and seemed to fall almost straight down.

The last thing he thought before he hit was, some farmer is going to be mad as hell at me for tearing up his crop.

Then the plane hit and went jerking and bouncing violently through the corn field. For a time China could see nothing; his windscreen was a sea of green as the corn stalks flew in all directions. He held on as best he could, but he was being violently pitched back and forth, first forward into his safety harness and then backwards into the seat. He tried to hold on to the wheel, but it pumped and jerked in his hands, then finally broke loose and slammed him in the chest. The rudder pedals were jumping up and down, hammering against his feet and legs.

Then the plane suddenly broke out of the corn field and China could see the meadow, with startled cattle staring at him. The plane had slewed around to the left, so the right wing tip was out in front. Still being thrown wildly about in his harness, he could hear the sudden grinding and shrieking of metal as the belly of the airplane struck the rocks in the field. A small tree caught the tip of the right wing and the airplane was jerked abruptly in that direction. The sudden shift threw China to his left. He banged his head hard against the window.

Finally the airplane seemed to be slowing. It bounced

and grated over a few more rocks, tore down another tree, and then slid grudgingly to a stop.

Battered, bruised, and stunned from the blow on the head, China unsnapped his harness the instant the plane stopped and staggered down the companionway to the door. For an instant he thought the crash had jammed it, but he tugged harder on the handle and it came loose. He threw the door open and sprinted from the plane. Only when he was a good fifty yards away did he stop and look back.

It did not catch fire, which surprised him. He suddenly sat down on the little grassy knoll he'd run to. He got out a cigarette and lit it with a slightly shaky hand. "Well," he said aloud, "got away with another one. You got a little skill and a lot of luck, cowboy."

He sat there smoking and staring at the airplane, cooling out. The airplane was a wreck. The starboard engine had been knocked loose from its mounts and now hung straight down from the wing. Most of the port wing tip was gone, and so was the port elevator. China didn't even see it anywhere. He marveled that, as battered and twisted as the airplane was, the cargo door had opened. But it had, even though there really hadn't been any rush. It hadn't caught fire, but it should have. He was sure that, with as many rocks as they'd skidded over, enough sparks had been raised to have started a thousand fires.

When he finished his cigarette, he got up and started toward the plane to retrieve the gear he'd left in his haste to get out. After his first step he realized he'd hurt his ankle. He sat down and pulled off his boot. His boot was cut and there was a gash on the inside of his anklebone. Something had hit it. With all the banging around he'd taken, he knew he was going to be sore as hell tomorrow.

He limped on over to the plane, climbed in and went forward and retrieved his flight kit and his instrument case.

He had left the rest of his stuff back at the motel in Laredo, a place that now seemed a thousand miles away. There didn't seem to be anything else he wanted from the airplane, so he went back down the companionway, crunching the glass from the TV sets under his boots. He got out again and then walked back up to the same knoll and sat down to consider what to do.

Before he did anything else, he took out the bottle of brandy from his flight kit and had a long pull. It burned good going down and he could feel it going to work as soon as it hit his stomach. Then he got out his first-aid kit and doctored and bandaged his ankle.

After that he sat a while more, smoking and sipping at the brandy. A few of the skinny Mexican cattle had wandered back after being frightened off by the plane. They stood a hundred yards away, still staring at him. He thought: I wonder what the hell goes through a cow's mind when a large airplane suddenly comes dropping out of the sky?

He glanced over at the corn field. It was pretty well devastated. An airplane, he thought, can do an amazing amount of damage to a corn field. There's probably a law of physics that applies to that in a book somewhere.

He knew he was feeling a little giddy, partly from the cognac and the knock on the head, but mostly from relief at having walked away from another one.

But it was all in a day's work.

Of course, this day's work wasn't going to pay as he hadn't delivered the goods.

He raised the bottle of cognac in a mock salute. "Satisfaction guaranteed. That's our motto. No play, no pay. And old Gomez didn't get no play for his money. So this crash is on me. On the house."

He took another drink of brandy, then corked the bottle and put it back in his flight kit. At the moment he wasn't quite sure what to do. Best he could figure, he was a good sixty or seventy miles overland from the border. Conceivably, if there were any towns close, he could make it in to one and arrange some sort of transportation back. But he didn't much like that idea. It was too risky. He had little doubt that there was a police alert posted for him, and with a hurt ankle and a gash and bump on the side of his head he would look very much like an out-of-place gringo. And he reckoned that any out-of-place gringo in this neck of the woods would come under suspicion as the pilot who'd tried to land a load of illegal contraband. He knew that the odds were long on his being picked up, but capture meant certain jail and that was a game he didn't want to draw cards in. No, he'd investigate some other possibilities first.

There was, for instance, the house that he'd seen only a little over a quarter of a mile away. He hadn't had the time to see if there were any vehicles there, but the quick impression he'd gotten had been of whitewashed walls and a red tile roof, with other little outbuildings scattered around. Conceivably someone who could help him lived there, but he needed to think out a story before he went trudging up to some stranger's front door. Could be the police chief lived there.

He was sitting there, trying to concoct a plausible explanation for his presence, and especially for a ruined airplane full of TVs and stereos, when he heard a slight noise behind him. He'd started to turn when a voice in English said, sternly, "Goddamit! Get your hands up! I got a shotgun!"

Without turning, he slowly raised his hands and came to his feet as he did. All he could think of was that the voice spoke English without an accent, so he had to figure it wasn't the police. He expected it was the owner of the corn field.

The voice said, "Now, turn around, dammit, and ex-

plain why you have seen fit to tear the livin' shit out of my
corn field with your goddam airplane!''

With his hands still in the air China turned slowly on his
heel. There, about twenty yards away, was a white-haired
old man in an undershirt and a pair of dirty overalls. But
there was no dismissing the business-like shotgun he held
leveled down on China.

China started apologizing right off. ''I'm sorry about
your corn field. I had no choice.'' He studied the old man,
trying to figure out what he could say that would get that
shotgun pointed in some other direction. It was a double-
barreled model, old but looking extremely serviceable, and
he could see that both hammers were cocked and that the
man had his finger inside the trigger guard. From that
range a blast would cut him in two.

''You're damn right you're sorry!'' the man said. ''But
you ain't half as sorry as you're fixin' to be.''

''Listen,'' China said, ''take it easy, will you? I'll pay
you for your corn field. I didn't want to be here anymore
than you wanted me to. But that airplane was coming
down and there wasn't anything I could do about it.''

''You could have landed somewhere else. Damn your
eyes!''

China said, ''Man, look around you! You see any place
else where I could have landed and had any chance of
surviving? I—''

''That's where you are wrong, bub. I don't give a damn
if you'd of survived or nay! I just didn't want you in my
corn field!''

China stared at him. It seemed as if he were dealing
with a man who put a corn field before human life. Well,
that shouldn't surprise him over much; he knew a lot of
people who didn't put much stock in human life. He said,
''Look, I'll give you whatever money you could have
gotten for this crop.''

"Yeah? You gonna pay me for them years I sweated to make it *into* a corn field? Clearing it? Cartin' off rocks by the truck load? Me and my wife was going to eat on that corn through the winter. And now look at it! What are we gonna eat now? You tell me that, mister smart-aleck flyboy who ain't got no respect for other people's property!"

"I—" China began. He was going to try and apologize again, but a thought suddenly struck him. He turned and looked at the corn field, especially where it joined the cow pasture. Then he turned back to the old man. "You say you and your wife was going to eat on that corn through the winter?"

"*Was,* mister smart aleck! Was! But not no more, not since you've done your work."

China said flatly, "You're a damn liar old man."

The old man gave him a startled look and raised the shotgun slightly. "You better watch your mouth, bub."

China said, "You and your wife weren't going to eat off that corn. There ain't even a fence between it and your cattle pasture. That corn was nothing but forage for your cattle."

The old man got red in the face. He said, "It's none of your goddam business what that corn was for. Fact of the matter is, you tore it up. That's all you better concern yourself about."

China said, "Put that shotgun down and let's talk." He lowered his hands.

The old man brandished the shotgun. "You better get them hands back up. This thing touches off mighty easy."

China said, "That thing goes off, you're in trouble. There'll be people looking for me and you'll have a hell of a time explaining how I come to get shot."

"You attacked me! You threatened my life."

"Bullshit! Listen," he lied, "the government knows my flight path and they're probably looking for me right now.'' On reflection, he thought, he probably wasn't lying after all. He said, ''So if you want big trouble you just let something happen to me. Now put that shotgun down!''

The old man was regarding him suspiciously. ''You work for the government? You work for the Mexican government? Then show me some cards or some credentials of some kind.''

''I never said I worked for the government. But because of this load of material I have, they are mighty interested in what happens to me.''

''Yeah? That brings to my mind to ask you just what you was doing flying around here in the first place. Ain't no airplanes ever come over this way. How come *you* was coming over here?''

China said, ''Look, that's a long story. Why don't you just put that shotgun down and let's you and I have a talk.'' He started forward.

The old man's voice got shrill. ''Just hold it right there, bub! Just stop where you are!''

But China kept going, walking slowly and deliberately, his hands at his side. ''Look, I'm tired of you pointing that thing at me. It could go off by accident, but I'd be just as dead. I don't mean you any harm. But I'm hurt and lost and I need some help.''

He was keeping up a steady stream of talk as he walked toward the man.

He said, ''You've got nothing to fear from me. But you better not shoot me or you'll really be in trouble. Like I say, the government is probably searching for me right now. Now put the gun down. I'm going to pay you for your corn. But I need help.''

He was within a few yards of the old man. The shotgun stayed relentlessly pointed at his chest. The old man had thrown it to his shoulder and China could see his eyes as they sighted down the barrel. The old man said, his voice shriller, "I'm tellin' you, stop where you be!"

China said, "You're going to make some money off this. You can use some money, can't you?"

China was up to the old man. He stopped. The shotgun was six inches from his chest. He suddenly put out his hand, grasped the barrel and tore the weapon away. The old man took a step backwards, looking alarmed. China broke the shotgun, ejected the two shells, put them in his pocket, and handed the gun back.

"Listen," he said, "I told you I don't mean you any harm. And I'll pay you. But right now I need some help to get back to Texas."

The old man was regarding him sullenly, standing there with the useless shotgun grounded by his leg. He said querulously, "Well, how the hell am I supposed to know you didn't mean to kill us all? Come flying in here tearing up a man's property, what am I supposed to think? For all I knew, you was one of them dope runners, one of them addicts, all hopped up on cocaine or whatever that stuff is. Man's got a right to protect his life and his property."

China said, "I'm not a dope addict. Or a dangerous man of any kind. I'm a professional pilot and I've had some bad luck and I need a little help. That's all."

The old man was still regarding him with hostility. "Well, if you're such an upstanding citizen, what about you was going to pay me for the damage you done to my land and corn?"

China had about six hundred dollars in his billfold and the thousand in emergency money in his flight kit. He pulled out his billfold, shielding it so the old man couldn't see how much he had. He took out three one-hundred-dollar bills. "As good as done," he said. He held out the money. The man reached out and took it dubiously. At close range, China could see he wasn't as old as he had first appeared. He was tall and scrawny, but there was nothing of an old man in his movements. China guessed him to be in his mid-fifties.

The old man looked at the money in his hand. He said, "Three hundred dollars? That ain't much."

"Okay," China said. He handed the man another hundred. "How's that?"

The old man still looked surly. He shaded his eyes and looked toward his corn field. "Awful lot of corn tore up out there."

China said, "It's just knocked over. Your cattle will still eat it. In fact, I ought to charge you for making silage out of it."

The old man glanced at him quickly and China figured he was surprised that he'd known what silage was. He said, "Oh, yes, I'm a country boy. I know about corn and cattle."

The old man looked off in the distance. He said, "Still, four hundred dollars . . ." He let it trail off.

"All right," China said. He handed the man two fifties. "Here's another hundred. And five hundred dollars buys a hell of a lot of corn. Especially since your cattle are going to eat it anyway."

The old man stuffed the money in his pocket. Then he waved his hand toward the airplane. "But what in hell am I supposed to do about that? That airplane? Sittin' there like an eyesore right in the middle of my cow pasture."

"Listen," China said, "when I get back to Texas and get word to the man that owns that airplane, he's going to send down here and get it."

"That big thing? How the hell's he going to get it out of here? It damn sure ain't going to fly without a hell of a lot of work."

"They'll cut it up," China said. "Take it apart and load it on trucks. Look, I told you there was going to be some money in this for you. When they come for the plane, you can charge the man as much as I've already given you for keeping it on your land for him. That airplane's worth a lot of money." Of course, that was a lie. The airplane wasn't worth anything. But the merchandise inside it was, and China felt sure Gomez would want to take a chance on coming after his electronic goods. There had to be at least forty or fifty thousand dollars' worth in the cargo hold.

The man said, "Well, I don't know. Seems I been put upon here and I ain't got no way of knowing if anybody's going to come for that airplane or not."

"For Christ's sake!" China said. "Listen, that airplane is loaded with radios and TVs. Go down and take your pick. There's a ton of them in there. And most of them are probably still in good shape."

"Yeah? TVs, huh?" He shifted his eyes to the airplane for a moment and then came back to China. "What make?"

"What?"

"What make? What brand?"

"What make? How the fuck do I know!" China stared at him in amazement. "A TV is a TV."

"Not necessarily," the man said. He scratched at his scraggly beard. "I used to sell TVs. Mostly handled RCA, which I figured was as good as any. But if you had RCA, the goddam public wanted Zenith. If you had Zeniths, the goddam public wanted RCA. Goddam public, drive a man crazy."

"Look," China said, "we can talk about this up at your house. I saw it from the air. But right now I'm a little hurt and tired and a hell of a lot thirsty. And it's hot as hell out here. Let's go up to your house and find some shade."

The man glanced away and scratched at his beard again. "My house? Well, I don't know about that. I got my missus up there and strangers might scare her."

"I'm not going to scare your wife," China said. "I'll

act just as nice as if I was in Sunday School. But I got to get in out of this sun. It's about to fry my brains. Have you got a phone up there?''

"What? A telephone? Hell, no. Bub, you're out in the boondocks. There ain't no phones around here. And I wouldn't have one if I could.''

"Okay, we'll worry about that later. But I've got to have a drink of water. You do have water, don't you?''

The man seemed to think a moment, staring off into the distance. Finally he said, "Well, I guess so. I guess it'll be all right. But you watch yourself around my wife, you hear?''

"Of course," China said. "Of course. Just let me step back down to where I was sitting and get my gear.'' He turned and limped back to where he'd left it. He called over his shoulder, "Now don't you load that thing again.''

He grabbed up his two bags and came limping back. The old man was standing as he'd left him. China was so thirsty he had cotton in his mouth. "Okay," he said, "let's go.''

It was uphill most of the way to the house. As they walked, the man said, "Name's Humboldt. Charlie Humboldt.''

China said his name. The man looked around at him. "I know," China said, "it's an unusual name. But it's the best I can do.''

Humboldt said, "Been here four years. Used to be in the appliance business in Tulsa, Oklahoma. One day I just chucked it and moved off down here.''

China said, "Why'd you do that?''

The man looked around at him, his face suddenly getting an angry cast. "The goddam public, that's why. I got so goddam tired of the goddam public that there just come a day when I figured if I had to see another of them idiots, much less have to deal with them, that I was going to pitch a fit! So I came way down here to get away from people in general and the goddam public in specific.'' He looked around at China. "And then you come dropping in out of the sky in your goddam airplane.''

"Just consider me a corn buyer,'' China said. "You sold your crop a little early.''

The old man rubbed at his beard and said nothing.

The house looked about as it had from the air, a little square structure of whitewashed cinder blocks with a red tile roof. China wondered what Humboldt did for water and electricity, but as they approached, he saw a little shed out back with wires running to the house and he assumed the man had a gasoline-fired generator.

So he was fixed up for solitude and he was eccentric as hell. And China couldn't count on him responding to normal motivation and logic. But he did appear to be greedy. That was good; that was a lever China knew he could pull to get the old man to do what he wanted him to.

He said aloud, "I guess businessmen just never lose the profit motive.''

The old man looked around at him sharply. "What's that supposed to mean?''

"Nothing,'' China said. "I'm a businessman myself.'' He said it thinking that Bonnie would rejoin, "Yeah, you're in monkey business.''

Humboldt said, "Well, I don't know. All I know is a man ain't ever going to go broke taking a profit.''

The house was just ahead. China said, "Well, if I don't get a drink of water pretty soon, I'm not going to care if I'm broke or not. By the way—'' He gave the old man a look. "What are you selling water for? By the glass?''

"You making sport of me?'' There was a little heat in Humboldt's voice and China told himself to bear in mind that the old man did not have a great sense of humor.

China said, "No, I'm making fun of myself for getting into such a sorry mess."

Humboldt said, "What happened to your airplane?"

China shrugged. "The engines quit running. Water in the gas tank or something." He suddenly thought of the bullet holes in the wing and the fuselage. They would have been a little hard to explain if the old man had insisted on going down and taking a look. It had been a slip on his part. He'd have to think of some way to keep the old man away from the airplane until he was long gone.

There was a veranda roof out from the front of the house and the shade felt very welcome as they stepped up to the door. The old man opened it and went through first, half closing it behind him. Humboldt yelled, "Claudie, Claudie! They's a stranger here!"

Then he opened the door and China stepped through. The room was cool and dim. It looked to be the living room. There was a hard bench couch with some cushions on it and two or three straight-backed chairs scattered around. It was all Mexican furniture, big and wooden and heavy. Over in the corner was a table that China figured was used for dining. It had a bench on each side. A single, bare light bulb hung from the ceiling. There was nothing on the walls. In the corner was an old roll-top desk. The floor was concrete with one small rug in the middle. A door led off to the right and at the back of the room was another, open so that China could see that it led to the kitchen.

A woman suddenly appeared in the kitchen door. It took a second for China's eyes to adjust, and then he could see that she was young, maybe in her mid-twenties. She was dark-skinned and dark-haired, but her face didn't look Mexican. She was pretty in a cheap, too made-up way— though China couldn't figure what the hell she was doing with make-up on way out in the sticks; habit, he reckoned—

but her figure was the kind that made men's throats get a little thick. She was wearing a loose skirt, but he could see the swell of her hips, going into a small belly. And, even across the dim room, he could see the way her firm breasts pushed against the material of her clothes. She was wearing a peasant blouse and it had fallen down over her shoulders.

She glanced at China and then at Humboldt. "What you want, Charlie?"

"This man wants some water. Bring him a pitcher and a glass. And put something over your shoulders, for Christ's sake."

Charlie put his shotgun in a corner of the room and then sat down on the couch. He motioned for China to take a seat in one of the chairs. The girl had disappeared into the kitchen. Humboldt said, "Before you say anything, that's my wife and not my daughter."

China shrugged indifferently.

Humboldt gave him a hard look. "You think there's something wrong with me having a young wife? You think I'm too old?"

"Oh no" China said. "No, no, no. You look like a man who deserves the best."

Humboldt sat on the couch cracking his knuckles. "Found her in Laredo a little less than a year ago. Married her." He looked over at China. "Man gets lonesome out here by himself."

China nodded. "There's that. And a man needs a woman to tend to things. Cooking and washing clothes."

The old man said, "Hah! Not her."

China had been trying to be folksy. Now all he could say was, "Oh." But he should have known by looking at the girl that she was no house frau. She looked like she'd be more at home in a whorehouse or cheap bar.

The woman came back in just then and set a pitcher and

two glasses on the table in the corner. Then she left without another glance at China. But he noted that she'd wrapped a shawl around herself. He heard a door in the back open and shut.

Humboldt nodded toward the water. "Help yourself."

"Thanks," China said. He crossed the room and poured out a glass of the cool well water and downed it without taking the glass from his lips. He poured another and drank that by halves. "Ah," he said, "you never miss the water till the well runs dry. Goddam, that tastes good!" He poured another glass and then returned to his chair, sipping at it. His flight kit was beside the chair and he rummaged in it and took out the bottle of cognac. He offered it to Humboldt, but the old man looked disapproving and shook his head. "Never held with liquor. Interfered with business."

"Yeah," China said, pouring some in his half glass of water. "That's the way I feel. You understand, I'm just taking this medicinally for my hurt ankle and this cut on the side of my head. Otherwise, I wouldn't touch it myself."

He took a long drink of the cognac and water, letting it slide down his throat and approach his stomach. After a minute he could feel it warming and relaxing him. Boy, he thought, am I going to be sore tomorrow from bouncing all over that cockpit. He could already feel a few places starting to hurt that he hadn't been aware of until he'd sat down and got relaxed.

The old man looked at his watch. He said pointedly, "It's nearly noon."

The time startled China. It seemed like about fifteen minutes ago that the Mexican police had been shooting at him. And just a little more than that since he'd taken off from Laredo. But that wasn't the reason the old man was telling him the time. He poured some more cognac in his glass, took another drink, and said, "Yeah, and you're wondering when you're going to get rid of me. Is that right?''

"That's right. I told you, I come down here to get away from the goddam public. And you're the goddam public.''

"Okay,'' China said. "Where's the nearest telephone?''

"About twenty miles from here. The town of Progresso.''

"All right, you're going to have to go in and make a call for me.''

"The hell I am!'' Humboldt looked at him. "You want to make a phone call you hit that road and start walking. If you can walk four miles an hour, you can make it by dark.''

China shook his head. "I can't walk.'' He nodded his head at his ankle. "Not that far. My ankle is hurt.''

Humboldt frowned at him. "I got a truck. Maybe I could take you part of the way. But I hate to make that drive. Road is so rough it just tears the hell out of the machinery.''

China shook his head again. "No, you'll have to go in for me. I can't go into town.''

Humboldt gave him a look. "Can't go into town? Why not?''

"I just can't,'' China said. He'd been thinking about it ever since he'd gotten out of the wreck, wondering how he was going to get the hell out of this god-forsaken country when he didn't have any excuse for being there in the first place. Well, it was time to think of something. "Don't ask me,'' he said. "Just make that trip into town. I'll pay you. I'll give you a hundred dollars.''

But Humboldt was still regarding him suspiciously. "You in some kind of trouble?''

"Trouble? Well, let me see. I'm hurt. Not much, but more than I want to be. I'm in your house where you don't want me to be. I'm a long way from home. I've just wrecked an airplane and failed at a job that's going to cost me quite a bit of money. Yeah, I'd say I was in some kind of trouble."

But Humboldt said, "That ain't what I mean. How come you don't want to go into town?"

China said, "Well, you finally got the truth out of me. I'm a famous movie star and every time I go around the goddam public, they drive me crazy asking for my autograph. You can understand that."

Humboldt didn't laugh. "You're in trouble with the police, ain't you? That's why you don't want to go into town and make that call yourself. You're smuggling dope, just like I thought."

"No, you old fool," China said, "I ain't smuggling dope." It looked as if he were going to have to take the risk. All he could hope was that he hadn't misread his man. He said, "I'm smuggling TVs."

"You're doing what?"

"Smuggling electronic goods. TVs, stereos, radios. Hell, you were the appliance king of Tulsa, Oklahoma; you ought to be able to understand what I'm talking about."

The old man was peering at him, his brow wrinkled. "Why would you want to be smuggling TVs into Mexico?"

"Because of the high import duty. They are trying to develop their own industry, so they discourage imports with a high duty. Understand? It's a very lucrative business. That means profitable. So the police don't like you doing it. If you'll go down and look at my plane, you'll see that it's shot up. The police were waiting for me when I tried to land about a hundred miles from here."

He was watching his man, watching his face for reactions that he could trust. But all Humboldt did was scratch his beard and look thoughtful. He said, "No shit?"

"No shit," China said.

"And you say that airplane is loaded with TVs and radios and such?"

"Yes." China was watching him narrowly.

"But you say the police might be looking for you?"

"Look," China said evenly, "quit talking about the police. That makes me nervous and you don't want me to get nervous. All I'm telling you is that I want you to go into Progresso and make a phone call for me. I'll pay you for it."

The old man mulled it over, staring at the far wall. He said, "You said a hunnert dollars. That ain't nothing for that trip. It's twenty miles over the roughest roads you've ever seen. No sir, I wouldn't do it for any hunnert dollars."

"Then two hundred."

"No."

"Three hundred."

"No. I'll do it for five hundred."

"Goddammit!" China swore. "Listen, old man, I ain't looking to buy this goddam place of yours. I only got so much money. I can't give you five hundred. I've got to have some left for an emergency."

Humboldt said, "It appears to me you've got an emergency right now."

China didn't answer, just poured more cognac in his glass, decided there wasn't enough water, got up and went to the table and poured more out of the pitcher. He took a drink. Well, the man was right. He did have an emergency on his hands. But he said, "Listen, Humboldt, I know and you know that you're going to take $10,000 worth of electronic goods out of that airplane as soon as I'm gone. Just how the hell much do you expect to make off of one forced landing?"

Humboldt said stolidly, "I only got your word about them TVs. If they're really there, they's likely all busted to hell anyway."

"Some are," China said. "But not all of them. They were very securely tied down. Some of them got shot up.

But there was at least $50,000 worth of merchandise on that plane. Look, old man, it is to your advantage to have me gone. Then you can take what you want out of that airplane in your own sweet time. It'll be at least a week before the man that owns that stuff can get down here. And even when he comes, there won't be much he can say about what's missing because he's a smuggler himself.''

Humboldt snorted. "Hell, you being gone ain't got nothing to do with it. I can go down there and take them TVs out any time I want to. You're wanted by the police; you ain't going to the police. You couldn't do anything about it.''

China had turned to pour more water in his glass. He came slowly back around, his eyes narrowing and turning hazel. "Don't bet on that, Humboldt," he said softly. "Just don't bet on that.''

The old man held his eyes for a second and then looked away. He said, "Well, maybe that wouldn't be fair play. I wouldn't take advantage of you in your time of trouble. Maybe I will go in for you and make that phone call. I'll do it for four hundred dollars.''

China regarded him steadily for a moment. "This afternoon?''

Humboldt shook his head. "No. Can't do it.''

"Why not?''

"Because I ain't ready. It's a hard trip, better than four hours there and back, just on the road. I couldn't get back before dark and I ain't going to be on that road after dark. It takes hell's own kind of time to get a call through. No, sir. I'll go first thing in the morning.''

China considered. But then he didn't really have any choice. He said, "All right.''

"Let me see your money.''

He cocked his head. "You don't trust me?''

"I don't trust nobody.''

"Okay," China said. He went back to his chair, rummaged around in his flight kit, and came out with the thousand dollars in emergency money. He leafed off four one-hundred-dollar bills and handed them to the man. Humboldt was looking at the rest of the roll. China put it in his pocket. "That," he said, "is for the next emergency." Then he bent down and took the .357 Magnum revolver out of his kit. As the old man watched, he deliberately flicked the cylinder out, checked the load, snapped it back, then shoved the gun down in his waistband. He looked at Humboldt. "You see," he said, his voice silky, "I trust you. I've always got a little something for emergencies."

It was a long afternoon and evening. The woman never appeared, and if any lunch was served, he wasn't invited. Mostly he sat outside under a shade tree and drank cognac. When that was gone, he smoked cigarettes. Humboldt worked around the place, appearing every so often carrying a shovel or going to the shed with a pair of pliers. Once he disappeared for about an hour and China felt sure he'd gone down and inspected the contents of the airplane.

Just at dark Humboldt called him in. He said, with no welcome in it, "I guess you'll want to eat supper with us."

"Yeah, I'm hungry," China said.

They ate at the table with the benches on both sides. Humboldt and his wife sat side by side across from China. They had beans and cornbread and *cabaritto*—barbecued goat—washed down with well water. It was neither bad nor good. China suspected that Humboldt had fixed the meal. The woman—though they hadn't been introduced, he supposed her name was Claudie—glanced at him a few times, but never said a word. When the meal was over, the girl cleared the table and disappeared.

Letting out a huge belch, Humboldt took himself over to sit on the divan. He said, clearing his throat, "We go to bed early around here. You better write out what you want me to say in that phone call.''

China went to his instrument kit, got out a ruler and a pair of dividers, and began calculating his location on the chart. Then he began writing his message. After a moment he stopped and looked at Humboldt. ''Old man,'' he said, ''you got any old tires around here? You know, discarded old rubber tires?''

Humboldt looked up at the ceiling. ''Yeah, there's a few around here. Off my old truck. But I been meaning to have them recapped. Save a good bit of money that way.''

China said evenly, ''Humboldt, you try and charge me for those tires and I'm going to break your arm. And I mean that.''

Humboldt said in an injured voice, ''I wasn't plannin' on charging you for some old casings. I'm just pointing out that everything out here in the middle of nowhere comes mighty dear. Mighty dear.''

China went back to work on his note to Bonnie. He printed it carefully so that the man would have no trouble reading it. It said:

> BONNIE, I AM DOWN IN THE BACK
> WOODS OF MEXICO. THE MAN WHO
> IS READING YOU THIS NOTE IS MY
> LINK TO GET OUT. ACT IMMEDIATELY.
> CALL PLAYER. IF NO ANSWER CALL
> MAX. IF NO ANSWER CALL LYNN.
> ONE OF THE PILOTS MUST LEAVE LA-
> REDO BY 11 AM TOMORROW MORN-
> ING. TELL THEM TO RENT A CESSNA
> 152 BECAUSE OF THE SHORTNESS OF
> THE LANDING AREA. TELL THEM TO
> TAKE A CORRECTED HEADING OUT
> OF LAREDO OF 205 DEGREES. I AM 81

AIR MILES FROM LAREDO. TELL THEM
TO LOOK FOR A SMALL GREEN VAL-
LEY WITH A CORN FIELD. CRASHED
DC-3 IS THERE. I WILL BE BURNING
RUBBER TIRES FOR FURTHER IDENT-
IFICATION. TIME IS TIGHT. SO THAT I
WILL KNOW YOU HAVE RECEIVED
THIS MESSAGE TELL THE MAN YOU
ARE TALKING TO THE NAME OF MY
BLAZE-FACED
HORSE.

He finished and handed the note to Humboldt. "Can
you read that?"

The man studied it for a moment or two and then said,
"Yes, I can read, bub. But what's that about the name of
your horse? Don't you trust me?"

"Sure," China said. "I trust you." He turned so that
the butt of the .357 was clearly exposed. "Sure I trust
you," he said again.

Not too long after that Humboldt disappeared into the
back. But he returned in a few moments with two blankets
and a pillow. He said, "You'll have to make do on the
floor. We ain't got but the one bed."

"That's all right," China said. "I don't figure to sleep
much anyway." He took the blankets from Humboldt and
spread them over the small rug in the middle of the room.

Humboldt said, "I don't run that generator at night.
Fact of the matter is, it'll be running out of gasoline in the
next ten or fifteen minutes. So you got that amount of time
to get done what needs doing with light. I'll be up before
dawn and will likely leave as soon as there's enough sun
for me to see the road. Let me know if you think of
anything you want me to bring you from town."

When Humboldt was gone, China took his money and

the revolver and put them inside the pillow case. The old man seemed too chicken to try and rob him, but you never knew.

When the lights went out, he took off his boots and lay down. At first it was not cool enough for the covering blanket, but as the night wore on, the mountain air grew chilly and the one blanket was almost not enough.

China did not really sleep, just dozed off and on all night.

Chapter Four

Sometime in the morning he heard the generator start up. In a moment the back door slammed and then Humboldt came into the room as the overhead electric light bulb began to glow. China sat up, yawning and still half-asleep.

"Good morning," he said to the old man.

Humboldt just grunted. "Be some coffee in a minute. I guess you'll be wanting some."

"No," China said, "I won't." He got up and folded his blankets and laid them on the divan. He was very stiff and sore from the bruising and a night on the cold, hard floor. It was an effort just to move. His ankle was still sore as hell and the side of his head ached a little. The inside of his mouth tasted awful. He said to Humboldt, "I'd like a glass of water and a little salt."

The old man said, "There's water in the kitchen and salt on the table. What the hell do you want with salt?"

"Clean my mouth out. Ain't got no toothpaste."

After China completed a primitive toilette, Humboldt grunted, "You don't want no coffee?"

China shook his head. "Stuff's bad for you. I prefer beer in the mornings. You ain't got such a thing as a Coke do you?"

"A Coke? You mean a Coca-cola? I reckon not. Whoever heard of drinking soda in the morning." He shook his head. "You're a strange one, bub."

China thought that coming from Humboldt that was some sort of compliment. It was still chilly, and would be until the sun got up good. "When you leaving?" China asked.

"Soon as I drink this coffee. Ought to have some daylight just about then."

China went back into the living room and wrote his home phone number and area code down on the note Humboldt would take with him. He hesitated a moment, thinking of putting down the man's number in New York. In the end he didn't. It would have been a breach of their agreement. He just had to hope and pray that Bonnie was home and wouldn't be outside or in the shower when the phone rang. He took the note and a twenty-dollar bill in to Humboldt. The old man looked at the note, folded it, and then took out a worn billfold and carefully put it inside. He put the twenty in also. "This for the phone call?" he asked China.

China said, "No, that's for whiskey. I want you to get me a bottle of brandy. If you can't get that, get rum; if they haven't got rum, get tequila."

"Going to get drunk, huh? I ain't sure I like that."

"No, I ain't going to get drunk. My ankle hurts and the side of my head hurts. I'm hoping some liquor will help."

"Well, what about the phone call? Where's the money for that?"

"Oh shit!" China said in disgust. "Humboldt, you are

the cheapest son-of-a-bitch I've ever known.'' He pulled another twenty out of his pocket. ''Now listen, old man,'' he said, ''you keep on trying that phone until you get her, you hear me?''

The old man was pouring himself a cup of coffee. He said, ''I'll do what I can.''

''No, not what you can. You get her on the phone. I know she'll be home. But I don't want you to miss her just because she's out feeding the horses or something. You reach her.''

Humboldt mumbled something and sipped at his coffee. China went to the sink and drew another glass of water. As he was drinking it, he said, ''By the way, what was all that yelling last night?''

Humboldt looked at him from under heavy eyebrows. ''What yelling? You must have been dreaming. I never heard no yelling. Could have been animal noises though.''

China said, ''I guess so.'' But he could have sworn that sometime during the night he'd heard little cries from somewhere.

Not too long afterwards Humboldt was ready to leave. ''When you going to be back?'' China asked him.

''Probably late this afternoon. Got a little business I can tend to while I'm in town.''

They went out the back door. It was just coming light in the east. Humboldt said, ''If you need anything to eat, help yourself to what you can find. My wife is going to stay in her room all day.''

China was surprised, suddenly realizing he hadn't seen her at all that morning. He said, ''She's not going with you?''

''No, she ain't,'' Humboldt said. ''But don't you let that give you any ideas, bub. You just stay plumb away from her, you hear?''

They had come up to Humboldt's old pickup, which

was parked just behind the house. China said, "Believe me, Humboldt, the only thing I'm interested in is getting out of here and getting back to my own woman. I won't go near your wife. I don't want any of that kind of trouble."

"You see that you don't." He opened the pickup door, then stopped before getting in. "Come to think of it," he said, "why don't you just stay outside until I get back. Get what you might need to eat and just stay outside. There's a faucet comes off the pump over yonder where you can get water."

"All right," China said, "I'll stay out of the house. You don't have to worry about me and your wife. Just make that phone call so I can get out of your hair."

"I can hardly wait," Humboldt grunted. Then he got in the pickup and slammed the door.

China leaned in the open window. "Now let me give you one warning, Humboldt. Don't bring the police back here with you."

In the growing light China could see the old man frown. "I got no such idea. I ain't even going to speak to the police."

"See that you don't," China said evenly. "Because if you do, there are two things that will happen and both of them are bad for you. One, if you bring the police back they will take the TVs and you won't make any money. And two, I'll kill you. I'll kill you dead."

The old man looked startled. He glanced quickly at China, then looked straight ahead out the windshield. "I damn near believe you would," he said.

"You better believe it," China said. "And you won't be the first. Remember, old man, you'll never go broke taking a profit, especially on TVs from heaven, so to speak. And you'll never get dead by my hand if you don't cross me. Now you have a good trip and drive safely."

Without a word the old man started the pickup, put it in gear, and drove off, lurching and jumping just a little.

Got a worn clutch, China thought as he watched the pickup out of sight. Hope the clutch holds out for one more trip.

It was going to be a long day. He got his gear from the house and then went out into the front yard as he'd said he would. He sat down on a prominent rock and lit a cigarette. It wasn't only going to be a long day—it was going to be a sweaty one. He wasn't too worried about Humboldt telling the police anything. The old man was too hungry for the TV sets and radios to risk losing them to the police. No, he'd make the call. But what China was going to have to worry about was him reaching Bonnie. If he got hold of her, it'd be all right. She'd find a pilot, of that he was certain. Lord, let her be at home, he prayed. Don't let her decide to have gone shopping or visiting on this particular morning.

If he didn't reach her, China didn't know exactly what he'd do. About his only other alternative was to bribe Humboldt somehow into taking him up close to the border. But he didn't much want to try that. To begin with he doubted if he had enough money. If a trip of twenty miles into town cost four hundred dollars, God knows how much a trip to the border would cost. Probably I don't have enough money in the world for that, China thought.

China decided to go down and have a look at the airplane while it was still cool. It was good light now and, except for his sore ankle and other bruises, it was pretty easy walking. As he got about halfway down the hill he could see that Humboldt's cattle were into the corn. He half grinned, thinking of how he'd almost fallen for Humboldt's line about how he and his wife were going to have to eat off that corn all winter. What a liar. And what a lazy farmer. If Humboldt had any sense, he'd shuck that corn somewhere and let it cure and dry. It'd have about twice the nutritional value as it did green.

He watched the cattle foraging through the high corn. You could turn cattle in to a corn field. They'd eat until they were full and stop. But you couldn't do a dumb horse that way. A dumb horse would keep on eating until he foundered himself. Foundered and died.

Still, he wished he was back in Texas feeding his dumb horses instead of wandering around a hillside in Mexico. One of these days he was going to founder himself, on chance-taking. Founder and die.

It was a nice morning. Even in the barren countryside he could hear the chirp of birds and insect noises. Ahead of him a gila monster slithered across a rock; the cold-blooded animal moved slowly, waiting for the sun to heat him into animation.

China hoped that the phone call would not scare Bonnie overly much. It would scare her a little, but that simply couldn't be helped. Well, he missed her—missed her a little more than he was willing to admit to himself, much less to her. A man in his profession had no business missing people because he had all too many opportunities to practice the habit.

He got to the plane and stepped up inside. After he'd looked around a second, he grinned to himself. Some of the cartons had been opened. It looked as if Mister Humboldt had been down inspecting the merchandise. He walked up to the cockpit. It didn't look any different, except he noticed two bullet holes in the floor—about a foot to the right of the pilot's chair. He whistled. He'd been shot at a little closer than he'd thought. A foot to the left and he wouldn't have been worrying about a phone call.

He sat down in the pilot's chair, turned on the master switch, and then tried one of the radios. It still worked. He sat a moment, listening to some air-to-air chatter and wishing he was in the air with a good plane under him; then switched the radio off. He wasn't planning on making any calls announcing his position.

He got up from the chair and went back outside. For a few moments he walked around the airplane looking at the damage. There were bullet holes everywhere. "Man," he said aloud, "they really sprayed me." In a way it was a miracle that the old, overloaded plane had managed to get off the ground and fly as far as it had. He patted it on the wing. "Thanks, old girl. I appreciate it. Sorry it had to end like this."

He walked back up to the house, his stiffness and soreness eroding a little with the exercise. He was getting hungry. He went back to the rock he'd been sitting on, rummaged in his kit bag and came out with a tin of dried beef. He opened it and then realized he'd forgotten to bring out any water or a glass. Well, he guessed he could go back in the house for that. The dried beef would be pretty hard going without something to wash it down.

He went in the front door. The girl was in the kitchen. He stopped at the door. "Oh, sorry. Just wanted to get a glass of water."

"That's okay," she said. She was wearing the same peasant blouse she'd had on the day before, only she'd changed the long skirt for a shorter one. The blouse had come off one shoulder again and he could see plenty of cleavage. She obviously wasn't wearing a brassiere.

She took a glass out of the cupboard and filled it from the tap and handed it to him, looking in his face as she did.

"Thanks," he said, turning away.

"Where you going?"

"Out front," he said, and walked out. He didn't want any of the kind of trouble he could see in her eyes.

He went back to the rock and sat down to eat the beef. He was plenty hungry and the meat tasted good.

He finished the meat and the water and then ate a chocolate bar. He was sitting there, feeling better, when the front door opened and the girl came out. She sat down on the ground in front of him, crossing her legs yoga fashion and making no attempt to watch her skirt which rode up on her legs until it was over her knees. He carefully looked away.

She said, "He didn't take me to town because he knows I'll run away if he gives me half a chance. He's got me trapped out here."

China was a little startled by the unsolicited announcement, but he only said, "I was wondering why he didn't take you."

"The old bastard. You got a smoke?"

"Sure," China said. He got out a cigarette, lit it, and handed it to her. She inhaled gratefully. "Old bastard won't let me have any cigarettes. Says they cost too much money. God, is he cheap!"

"I know," China said. He was still not looking directly at the girl. He wasn't sure where things were going, but he knew for sure this broad was trouble—and that was one thing he had enough of already. Women were strange creatures, he believed, capable of most anything, this one more than most if he reckoned right.

"He says the police shot your airplane down."

"Yeah."

"We heard it come over just before you landed."

"Crashed," he said. "Not landed."

"Whatever. I was really glad to see you come. God, I been going crazy around here. Talk about bored. I've been out of my skull."

China said, "If you hate it so much here, there ought to be some way you can leave."

She shook her head. "No way that I can think of. You don't have any more of what you were drinking last night, do you?"

He shook his head. "No. I wish I'd known you'd wanted some. You should have said something."

"Shit, I couldn't say anything to you. He'd of killed both of us. The old bastard is crazy as hell. If I'd of shown the least little bit of interest in you, he'd of never made that trip for you. I swore to him on my mother's grave I'd stay in the bedroom with the door shut all the time he was gone. God, I was never so glad in all my life to find out he was going and leaving me here alone with you."

"What makes you think he hasn't doubled back and is watching us right now?"

She shook her head. "I checked before I came out. Out the back a little way is a place where you can see the road as it goes around a mountain. I watched until I saw his truck. It's a good five miles by road to that point and he's not about to spend the gas to come back after he's gone that far." She cocked her head to one side. "Besides, he wants your money too bad. And on top of that, he's afraid of you."

"Good," China said. "That's just the way I want it."

She said, "You got another cigarette?"

"Sure." He lit her another one and then lay the pack and his lighter between them. Then he said, "Listen, it's none of my business, but if you feel like he's holding you prisoner, why don't you slip away or something. Get word to the police. I could do that for you."

She laughed without humor. "No, thanks. No police. That's the one thing the old bastard and I have in common—we don't cotton to the police. So don't worry about him bringing the law back here, because he knows the first thing they'd probably take is me."

"You got trouble with the police?"

"Yeah. That's what I'm doing here with that crazy old man. I been hiding out more than anything else." She hooked her arms around her knees and rocked back a little.

"So?" He drew on his cigarette and let her talk.

She said, "I got busted on a marijuana transporting charge. This jerk I was going with at the time got me to carry two pounds of good grass across the border. I got caught and that cocksucker got away. Never even bothered to see what had happened to me or try to get me out of jail or anything. I had to pay a bail bondsman the last of the money I had to get out on bail." She drew on her cigarette and then tossed her head back and blew the smoke toward the sky. "So I was out on the streets—you know, no money, no job. So I did what I had to to get by. I picked up Humboldt one night, and after he found out what the deal was on me, he said I ought to marry him over in Mexico and come back here and live. Shit, what did I know. With no money and a public defender for a lawyer I was headed for girl's school at the Seagoville prison." She paused to flick a bug off her smooth, tanned forearm. "And I don't like prison. I never been in prison, but I've been in jail a couple of times and I damn near couldn't stand it."

"So you married Humboldt?"

She shrugged. "Shit, I don't know if we're married or not. We saw some kind of a guy in Mexico and all that happened was we signed a paper. Wasn't no ceremony or anything."

"Didn't you read the paper?"

"It was in Spanish. What the fuck do I know from Spanish? All I wanted to do was get away from the border and away from the police and that jail. Besides, I didn't know Humboldt was nuts then. He seemed like a pretty nice old guy and he made this place back here sound like a vacation resort." She looked around her. "Some resort, huh? But he knew. He knew once he got me back here, there wouldn't be a fucking thing I could do."

"I see," China said. He felt sorry for the girl, but he didn't really know what to say to her.

"So even if I walk out of here, where do I go to? No money. How do I get to the border? Hitchhike? You can guess how long it would take the police to pick me up hitchhiking."

"How about Humboldt's truck? Can't you steal that?"

"Are you kidding? That old bastard keeps those keys hid, and even if I could somehow get it started, it's a stick shift and I don't know how to drive one of those."

China laughed in spite of himself. "How old are you, Claudie?"

"Twenty-four. Feel about forty."

"Well, listen," he said, "I can help you out on one part of it. The money part—not much but a little." He dug in his pocket and leafed off five twenties and held them out to her. "Here's a little. If you can get to a town, it'll buy you a bus ticket anyway."

"Hey, you don't have to do that."

"I want to." He flicked the bills. "Here, take it."

When she was slow putting out her hand, he just dropped it in her lap. "I guess you can keep that hidden from Humboldt, can't you?"

She cocked her head and looked at him. "Hey, you're a nice guy. You didn't have to do that."

"I told you I wanted to."

The sun was up good now and it was getting hot. China glanced at the sky, guessing it to be nine or ten o'clock. The girl said, "Listen, let's go in the house. It's cooler there."

China shook his head. "Best not," he said.

"Why not?"

"I told Humboldt I'd stay outside."

She gave a hoot of laughter. "You're kidding! What do you care about that old bastard? C'mon, let's go in."

He said, "No. And listen, don't think you owe me anything for that money. You don't."

She cocked her head at him again. In the light, without make-up on, she wasn't as cheap looking as she'd appeared the night before. And her body was still the kind that would make a man's throat tighten. She said, "Listen, it's not you I'm thinking about—it's myself. I'm horny as hell."

He was a little surprised. The old man wasn't that old. He said, "What about Humboldt?"

"Oh shit!" she said in disgust. "You know what he's into? Spanking my bare ass. That's how he gets his rocks off. Humboldt? Shit!"

"Spanks you?" China started to laugh and then he stopped and grinned narrowly. "So I *did* hear some screams last night. You were yelling."

"Yeah," she said. "I was. He was at it again. Usually I don't yell because that just turns him on worse. But I thought last night that if I yelled, he'd get embarrassed you'd hear and stop. But he wouldn't. I think all that money you gave him really had his head spaced."

China said, "I shouldn't laugh, but it's funny. The old bastard is kinky, huh? But does he hurt you?"

She shook her head. "Naw. I make him think he does, though, to keep him from going too far. I've had a hell of a lot worse done to me by men. My old man that I was living with who brought me to Mexico and got me busted used to get drunk on whiskey and knock the shit out of me." She lifted her upper left lip. Two teeth were missing. "He did that about a month before we came back to Texas. Fucking Mexican dentist nearly killed me getting out the parts that that cocksucker didn't break off when he hit me."

China felt sorry for her, but he didn't want to go to bed with her. She'd just been rode hard and put up wet too many times.

Abruptly, she moved toward him. She put her hands on the top of his thighs and looked up in his face. "C'mon, guy, let's go in. It's cool in the house."

China said, "Claudie, I'm a very happily married man. I don't fool around. It's that simple."

Still looking him in the face, she reached up with one hand and pulled her blouse off one shoulder, then the other, until her breasts were exposed. They struck out, young and firm and brown, with large dark red nipples. A little catch came in China's throat. But he laughed it down. "Look, I didn't say you weren't sexy. You're sexy as hell. But I told you I was married. Happily married."

"Feel it," she said. She took one of his hands and put it on her right breast. "It's me. It's not silicone. Men tell me I got the best tits they've ever seen that haven't been worked on."

"I think you're right," he said. He looked down at them, feeling a stirring inside in spite of himself.

She moved his hand over to her other breast and then took one of his fingers and carressed her nipple with it. Her breathing was coming faster and faster. She said, "C'mon, c'mon, let's go in the house."

When he didn't answer, she suddenly stood up and cupped one of her breasts in her hand and put it to his lips. He drew back slightly, but she followed him with the nipple. He kissed it and ran his tongue over it, caressing it lightly. It had become very erect and very hard. She sighed and shivered and took one of his hands and tried to put it underneath her dress. He pulled loose from her hands and stood up. "Look, Claudie," he said, "cool your jets. This is nothing but bad news for both of us."

She stood there looking at him, still panting slightly.

Finally she shrugged. "Okay. What the hell. But it ain't often I get turned down. In fact, you may be the first."

"I told you," he said, "I'm a happily married man and I don't cheat."

She sat back down on the ground and crossed her legs. But she made no attempt to put her blouse back up over her breasts. She said, "Bullshit." Then she looked at him shrewdly for a moment. "I bet I know what it is. You think I been around too much. You think I been handled by too many men. You think I'm some kind of tramp or hooker. You think if I had as many dicks sticking out of me as I've had stuck in me, I'd look like a porcupine. You think a classy guy like yourself is too good for me. That's it, ain't it?"

"Hell, no," China lied, a little startled at her perception. "I just don't screw around on my wife."

She gave a little bark of laughter. "Don't hand me that jive, sweetheart. Ain't nobody that married."

He didn't say anything, just lit a cigarette for her and one for himself. She took the smoke, inhaled deeply and blew the smoke toward the sky. "But I'll tell you this—I'm clean. I been here over six months and you can't get a dose of clap being spanked on the ass. So in case you change your mind . . ."

"Okay" he said. "I hear you."

But he really couldn't have cared less. He wasn't of the school that said, "Never turn down a piece of ass; you may never get another chance." In fact, he'd been culling ass ever since he was fifteen. Back on the professional rodeo circuit, where the shiny brights—rodeo groupies— were so thick you could stir them with a stick, he'd once told a buddy, "Hell, I don't want a cow that's been milked to death—or a horse that's been rode to death. Besides, when you're as good-looking and talented as I am, you can just about take your pick." For that remark his colleagues, with whom he was bunking five to a room in a cheap motel, had shut him out and made him sleep in the pickup truck they were traveling in.

But Bonnie really had been on his mind when the girl was making her advances. In fact, he'd noticed lately that every time he got in a tight place, he got to thinking more of Bonnie than he should. To him that sort of an attitude weakened a man, put his mind somewhere other than on the troubles he had at hand. He was almost tempted to take the girl up on her proposition, just to prove to himself that Bonnie wasn't taking over too much of his thinking.

Claudie said, "What's it like to be a pilot?"

He half smiled. He'd been asked that before. "You can't explain it in words. You just have to get up there in the sky and see for yourself."

She looked wistful. "I wish I could do something— something besides spread my legs and take shit from everything in pants. Hell, I can't do anything."

There wasn't anything China could say to that. He wasn't much of a hand at giving people advice about their life. If they didn't know what they wanted and how to get it, he damn sure didn't.

She said abruptly, "Can I leave with you when the plane comes to pick you up?"

"No," he said.

"Why not?"

"Because the plane that's coming to pick me up is a two-seater and there'll be no room."

"I don't weigh much. Maybe a hunnert, hunnert and five."

"Shit, Claudie, I'd like to help you, but I don't see how I can. Besides, Humboldt is not going to let you get in that airplane with us. And you know he'll be down there, watching everything going on."

"You could knock him out," she said.

He shook his head. "C'mon, Claudie, don't put that load on me. I got enough troubles already. Are you even sure you ought to go back?"

"Hell, yes!" she said. She reached down and inspected one of her bare toes. "I'm going nuts here."

"You know the police will still be looking for you. And if you jumped bail, the bondsman's going to be looking for you even harder than the police."

"I don't care," she said. "I don't care. Anything's got to be better than this. Even prison. If I could just get back up north again, up to Chicago, I'd be all right. I've got a lot of friends there."

"But I'm going back to Laredo. That's where you jumped bond."

"But I could lay low there until I could get out of town. Christ, after all these months they won't be looking for me there."

"I just don't see how I can do it," China sighed.

She gave him a look. "Listen, don't worry yourself about it. I'll make out. I been on my own for ten years. And I don't need some big shot like yourself feeling sorry for me or telling me what to do."

She went back in the house after that. It grew increasingly hot and he moved into the puny shade provided by a stunted oak tree. It didn't help much. The sweat was running down his upper body and dripping off his eyebrows. He continually had to keep wiping it off with his sleeve to keep it out of his eyes. The only good he could think of from the heat was that it was baking the soreness out of him. His head still ached a little, though. He put up his hand and touched the tender area just above his temple on the left side. There was still a good-sized lump there and he could feel the jagged gash in the skin, rough with dried blood.

His greatest discomfort was the gritty, salty feeling of

his skin with all the sweat drying on him. He sat there in the hot afternoon, dreaming of getting back to his motel and taking a long, cold shower and then taking a nap between clean, cool sheets with the air conditioner going full blast.

The girl came out and brought him a plate of beans with some cornbread. But she didn't speak, and she was gone before he could think of anything to say.

Mostly he sat there worrying that Bonnie wouldn't be at home to answer the telephone. But if she wasn't, she wasn't, and he was just going to have to come up with an alternate plan. He thought about that as the afternoon dragged on and the sun got hotter. The best he could figure was that he was just going to have to take the old man's pickup and drive out. Claudie had told him that Humboldt always hid the keys. Well, if the news was that he hadn't reached Bonnie, then he'd simply have to make him cough them up—by whatever method. He hated to do it, but he would if it came down to it.

He took his plate back up to the house and set it just inside the door. In the dim of the room he could see Claudie sitting on the couch and staring straight ahead.

He said from the doorway, "You all right?"

"Yeah, sure. Everything's cool."

He started to turn away and she asked, "You're not going to tell Humboldt what I said, are you?"

"You kidding?" he said. "I'm not going to tell him we talked at all. As far as I'm concerned, I didn't even see you today."

She said, "There's a tank out back by the pump shed. You can take a shower under that if you want."

"Thanks."

Behind the pump shed he found a fifty-five-gallon drum set up some eight feet on wooden stilts. He could see a hose line running to it from the pump house. Just under and connected to the bottom of the drum was a big shower head with a chain pulley. He got out of his boots and clothes as fast as he could and stepped under the drum and pulled the chain. The cold water came cascading down like a long-awaited relief. There was no soap, but he ran his hands over his skin, doing his best to wash off the accumulated sweat salt. Then, for a long, pleasurable few minutes, he just stood under it and let the coolness rain down on him. He didn't leave until the drum was empty.

The relief was short-lived, lasting only until he put his sweat soaked clothes back on. But, as he reminded himself as he struggled into his clinging shirt, this was all in a day's work for him.

Claudie was sitting outside the back door of the house as he came around the pump house. She said, "Hey, man, I didn't mean to put no load on you. I can handle whatever I'm into, you understand?"

"Yeah," he said.

"So don't worry about me. Okay?"

"Okay," he said. "I wasn't worrying."

"And if you want your money back, that's okay."

"I don't want the money back. Just put it to good use." He walked around the house and sat back down under the little oak tree. He looked up, gauging the sun in the sky. It had to be at least five o'clock. He wished mightily that Humboldt would get back. He looked at his watch and was disappointed. It was only a little after three. He still had a bit of waiting to do. God, he hoped Bonnie came through.

The afternoon dragged on. He dozed a little, sleepy after the long night he'd spent on the concrete floor. The girl did not come out again, for which he was grateful. She had gotten to him, making him wish he could do something for her.

He dozed a little more, then suddenly came awake to the sound of a motor somewhere off in the distance, but carrying through the quiet of the highland air. He stood up, looking toward the sound. The land fell away to the right of the house and, looking hard, he could see flashes of Humboldt's yellow painted truck as it chugged uphill over the road. After a moment or two the truck came into plain sight. Humboldt turned it left at the clearing around his house and then, without a glance at China, drove on around behind the house. China went hurrying after him.

He got up to the side of the truck just as Humboldt was killing the engine. He got out of the cab without a word and put the keys in his pocket.

China said, "Well?"

Humboldt gestured at the bed of the pickup. "You wanted some old tire casings. I picked some up in Progresso." He looked satisfied. "I figured you was going to burn them for a marker. I got these worthless ones for that. That way, I get to keep the ones I got that can be recapped. Did I figure it right?"

China said, "Fuck the tires, what about the phone call?"

Humboldt gave him a sour look. "Your blaze-faced horse is named Lucky."

China sighed. "So you got through to her. She answered the phone."

"That she did," Humboldt said. "And I tell you, that wife of yours can ask more questions in one minute by the clock than I can answer in an hour."

"But you read her everything I wrote? You read it all to her?"

"Hell, yes," Humboldt said. He reached in his shirt pocket and took out the slip of paper and handed it to China. "Here it is. I read it all, just like you wrote it down." Humboldt went past him. "Now get your goddam tire casings out of my truck. I done hauled them far enough for you as it is."

As Humboldt disappeared into the house, China just stood there feeling relief. With luck he was going to be out of this mess in less than twenty four hours.

Humboldt did not reappear for two hours, and then only to call China to supper. The sun was nearly down and the meal and the bedtime were a repetition of the night before. Claudie neither looked nor spoke to him and disappeared into the back as soon as she'd cleared the table.

Humboldt lingered a few minutes more and then went to fetch the two blankets and a pillow. He said, "You didn't bother my wife none today, did you?"

"No," China said, "I didn't bother your wife."

"Damn good thing," the old man said. "If I thought you had, there'd be trouble."

China felt a sudden spurt of anger. He was tired of the old man and disgusted with the way he treated the girl. He said, "Listen, old man, I've eaten your food and drank your water and slept on your floor. But I've paid plenty for them and I ain't exactly a guest. There's a plane coming for me tomorrow, so you get it straight in your mind that if there's any trouble, I'll be the one to finish it. Now get out of my sight before I harm you. You're too little for me to hit, but I'm liable to slap the shit out of you!"

The old man looked at him a second and then whined, "You can't talk to me like that."

China said, "Just shut your yap, old man, before I shut it for you. And where's the whiskey I told you to bring me?"

Humboldt got a crafty look on his face. "Well," he said, "since you're such hot shit, why don't you figure it out for yourself?"

In three steps China had him by the neck of his shirt. He half lifted him off the concrete floor. "Old man, I asked you where the whiskey was I gave you the money to buy.

Either give me the money back or tell me where the whiskey is.''

The grip China had on him was strangling the old man. He said, gasping a little, ''In the truck seat. Goddam!''

China let him back down and released his hold. ''It better be,'' he said.

The old man turned away, brushing down the front of his shirt. ''Can't take a little joke.'' Then he shuffled out of the room.

China went out in the night and walked around the house to the truck. He opened the door and searched around on the seat until he found the bottle. Then he took it back in the house. The light was still on, though it was beginning to go dim as the generator ran down. China looked at the bottle—it was brandy, but the cheapest Mexican kind. Well, he hadn't expected Remy. The old man would have to have made as much profit out of the twenty-dollar bill as possible.

He drank rapidly for the light was going fast. Just before it went out completely, he filled the glass with water again, picked up the blankets and the pillow and stepped out the front door. He didn't know what the old man was capable of, but he preferred to trust himself to whatever was crawling on the ground rather than sleep in Humboldt's house.

He found a cleared place beyond the stunted oak. There he put his two bags at one end, lay the pillow on them and arranged the blankets, then lay down with his glass of brandy and water. There was just a sliver of moon and the stars were very bright in the black sky. He lay there, sipping at the drink, and wondered what Bonnie was doing. It was too early for her to have gone to bed. Likely she was watching TV. No, more likely she was scrubbing the bathroom or the kitchen floor, as she always did when she was nervous. And he reckoned after that phone call she'd be pretty nervous indeed.

He was tired and a little sleepy. The ground, though still hard, seemed softer than the concrete floor. He finished his brandy and water and thought of Claudie, feeling bad that he couldn't help her. But hell, like she'd said, she was a big girl. She'd got herself in the mess and she was just going to have to get herself out the best way she could. Even if she could get away from Humboldt long enough to get in the airplane, a Cessna 152 still wouldn't safely carry three adults, especially considering the terrain they'd be taking off from. Hell, he had enough trouble on his hands without worrying about her. Man went to involving himself overly in other people's troubles and he'd end up not tending to his own business as well as he should.

Like the night before, he didn't sleep very well, just dozed off and on until dawn. In one of his periods of half-sleep he thought he heard the girl yelling again, but next morning, folding his blankets, he decided he'd just imagined it. Besides, she'd told him the old man didn't really hurt her. And she did look fine at the breakfast Humboldt grudgingly invited him to share. Still, as at supper, she did not look at him or speak.

Chapter Five

About eight o'clock the next morning he started transporting the old tires down to the cow pasture. In his note he'd said whatever pilot was coming should leave Laredo no later than eleven a.m. But they might come earlier and it was only an hour's flight, even in a Cessna 152, so he thought he'd go ahead and get his rubber tires to burning. They'd burn for hours.

It took him two trips. The old man came out and watched him. Suspicious old bastard, China thought idly. He lugged the tires to the upper end of the field, right where it quit being pasture and turned into sand and rocks. As he was bringing down the last two tires, the old man said, "Now that yahoo you got coming ain't going to land in my corn field again, is he? If it does, it's just going to cost you more money."

China didn't even bother to answer him.

Claudie had come out, too, and she watched as he rolled

the tires down the hill, letting them bounce and jump over the rocks until they fell on their sides. Then he'd catch up to them and start them rolling again. He still had about two-thirds of the bottle of brandy left, and he was trying to think of how to get that and some cigarettes to her without Humboldt catching on. It seemed the least he could do.

After he had the tires piled together, he drained some gas out of one of the wing tanks and poured it over them. He used a clump of dried grass as a torch, and in a little while the tires began to catch, sending up a trail of black smoke. Watching the fire, he noticed Humboldt coming down the hill. Claudie was trailing after him, some five yards back. The old man was carrying his shotgun, and China wondered if they were about to have at it again. But all Humboldt said was, "Just come to make sure you wasn't setting my pasture on fire."

China gave him a disgusted look. "Humboldt, green grass doesn't burn. And where it ain't green, it's sand and cactus and rocks and they don't burn either."

"Well, you just be careful with it."

"Listen," China said, "why don't you go count your TV sets and leave me the hell alone? I'm just about sick of you as it is."

"Aw, go fuck yourself. I'll be glad to be shut of you, I can tell you that."

Humboldt sauntered off toward the plane. Claudie stayed, waiting within talking distance of China. He waited until Humboldt had clambered up into the airplane before saying, "Listen, I got some brandy left. I'll leave you that and some extra packs of cigarettes in that clump of cactus yonder." He pointed with his chin to the pile of thick underbrush he was talking about.

She didn't look. She said, "You ain't going to take me with you when you go?"

He frowned. "Goddammit, I can't Claudie. Don't you understand it's just a little two seated airplane?"

"I could sit on your lap. It's not far to Laredo. Not by air."

He sighed. "Listen, it's not the number of passengers, it's the weight. I've told you, a 152 will barely carry two full grown adults, much less three. You can't just cram everything you can in an airplane and hope. It won't take off."

"It might," she said, a wistful note in her voice.

"Oh shit!" he said in disgust. "And if it didn't? There is very little opportunity to say overs when you're trying to get an airplane off the ground. Especially on terrain like this. Look, I'm sorry. I know you don't understand, but it would be too dangerous."

"He whipped me again last night," she said.

"So? You said it didn't hurt."

"Naw, he didn't whip me like he does when he's getting his rocks off. He whipped me to hurt me. With his belt. He was trying to make me admit we fucked."

"He's just bluffing," China said. "He doesn't know a goddam thing. He's just trying to get you to admit something he hopes isn't true. Just stick by your story. I told him I didn't even see you."

She said, "Well, I don't know what to do." She looked away.

He said, "What if I made him give you the keys to the truck? And then I held him long enough for you to get away. Could you make it?"

She shook her head and said, her voice toneless, "Naw, like I told you, I don't know how to drive a stick shift. And I didn't know any way out of here. There's a lot of little-bitty roads and you got to know which ones to take. Humboldt is the only one that knows."

"Hell, Claudie," he said, "I don't know what to tell you. Maybe I could come back for you."

She shook her head. "You wouldn't."

"Maybe I would."

"No, you wouldn't."

"All right, I wouldn't." He felt helpless, guilty and helpless. Though why he should feel guilty was more than he could figure. Hell, he hadn't gotten her into this mess. Finally he just said, "I wanted to let you know where I'd leave the brandy and cigarettes."

"Thanks," she said, still in that toneless voice.

Humboldt came out of the airplane. He was carrying something under his arm. From the looks of it China guessed it to be a portable radio. He walked back toward his house, yelling for Claudie to come on. She gave China the briefest of looks and then turned away and went trudging toward the old man, her head down. As she caught up with him, China could hear the old man asking what they'd been talking about. "You been talking about me behind my back to that man? Have you? You better not have been. I'll slap the shit out of you if you have."

China watched her fall in line behind him as they both went up the slope toward the house.

Well, he thought, it would soon be no problem of his.

If it ever had been.

A little later, when the tires were burning good and sending up a thick stream of black smoke, he glanced at his watch. It was nearly ten o'clock. Someone could be coming at any time. He needed to be ready.

Sweating and panting, he hurried back up the hill and gathered up his two bags. Then he took the glass that was still outside and went around to the pump and drew off a glassful from the faucet. He drank that, then filled the glass again and, carrying it in one hand and his two bags in the other, went on back down the hill. As he passed the house, Claudie was standing in the front watching him. He nodded at her without a word.

A little over an hour later he heard the faint sound of a plane. Because of the peaks all around, he could not tell which direction it was coming from, but he peered intently toward the northeast, toward Laredo, trying to see something that wasn't there.

Then he spotted a speck in the sky in that direction, and even as he watched, the speck grew larger. It came on and on until it began to take on the shape of an airplane. He still couldn't tell what kind it was, but he could see it beginning to lose altitude. It was still a good three or four miles away, but coming dead on course for his signal fire.

The plane came nearer, losing altitude until it was only a couple of hundred feet overhead. It came directly over the field, flying straight down the middle of the pasture, and China could see that it was a red and white Cessna 152. Damn, he thought, saved my ass one more time. The pilot cleared the end of the field and then turned back. He could see the direction of the wind from the smoke and could tell he'd have to land from the other end. China waved and the plane waggled its wings in recognition.

The plane turned on final approach and China watched approvingly as the pilot set up to land. China couldn't see who the pilot was, but he hoped it was Player. The plane dropped lower, gliding now, the power pulled. China could see he was using full flaps. The plane came in, just brushing the tops of the corn stalks with its wheels, and then it was flaring out for the landing in the cow pasture. It touched down, rolled a few feet and then bounced back up as it hit a rock structure, rolled and bounced again, slowed, and then settled down and came on at taxi power.

The plane drew up almost abreast of him, turned back and came around with a gunning of the engine. China went running over, stooping to duck under the high wing, his hair blowing in the prop wash. He jerked open the door, and Player sat there looking at him, half a grin on his face. He said disgustedly, ''Can't you stay out of trouble long enough for me to get any of my own work done?''

''What kept you?'' China asked in an aggravated voice. ''Goddammit, I was nearly out of whiskey, low on cigarettes and plumb out of women.''

Player nodded his head in a direction over China's shoulder. ''I don't know about the whiskey and cigarettes, but it don't look like you was out of women.''

China looked over his shoulder. Humboldt and the girl were standing some fifteen yards away, by his signal fire. He looked back at Player and then he looked at the girl again. For a second he stood there chewing his lip, thinking.

Player said, ''Goddam, get in here, will you? I get paid by the hour and you're running up a hell of a bill.''

He said, ''Set the emergency brake.''

''*What?*''

''Set the hand brake. *Do it!*''

China's eyes blazed hazel, and Player knew that this was no time to cross him. ''What the fuck,'' he said, and pulled on the hand brake. The he just stared impassively at China.

China said, ''Now get out on your side. You come with full tanks?''

''Yeah. Why?''

''Because we got to drain off ten gallons of gas.''

''Why? Hell, we got plenty of lift. I ain't gained that much weight. Have you?''

''Just do it.''

He pulled back out of the door and reached up under the wing for the petcock sump that drained the wing tanks. On the other side Player was doing the same. China let his run until he reckoned he'd jettisoned five gallons. He figured

Player had done the same. He yelled across, "That's enough! Get in, I'll be right back."

Ducking under the wing he ran back toward where his gear was sitting by the signal fire. Humboldt was standing there, his shotgun grounded by his leg. Claudie was standing next to him, watching China. Without a word China suddenly came up to the old man and grabbed the shotgun, wrenching it out of his hands.

"What the hell!" Humboldt yelled. He lunged toward China, but China shoved him away with one hand. He broke the shotgun, extracted the shells and pocketed them, and then hurled the shotgun into the underbrush.

Humboldt was standing there with his mouth open. China drew the .357 revolver out of his belt. He pointed it at Humboldt's belly. "Now get up to your house, old man. Get gone!"

The old man took a step backwards, so surprised he just opened his mouth and closed it.

China said, "Get gone! Now!"

The old man took another step backwards and then he found his voice. "What the hell you think you're doing! You got no right to—"

China fired a shot into the ground near the old man's feet. The bullet hit the hard surface and went whining away. Rock fragments sprayed into the old man's ankle and he suddenly jumped and howled.

China said, "Next one is in your leg! Now get!"

The old man stumbled backwards and then suddenly turned and ran, tripping and falling, scrambling and lurching, hell-bent to get back up the hill.

China stuck the revolver in his belt and then grabbed up his two bags. He motioned at the girl who'd been standing there, astonishment and dawning hope on her face. She said, "Do you mean you're taking me with you after all?"

"Yes, goddamn it all to hell, but we have to hurry.

Let's *go* now.'' He grabbed her by the hand and they went running to the airplane, ducking under the wing as they got to the door. Player was looking at him, shaking his head. China pulled the door open, crawled into the copilot's seat and pulled the girl in on top of himself. She was laughing and trying to hug him around the neck.

"Stop!" China said. "Goddammit, this is going to be a tight enough fit as it is."

Player said, "What the hell is this?"

"Tell you later. Let's get going." He was trying to shut the door, but Claudie's knees were in the way. He shifted her over to his left side, pulled the door shut and locked it. But her arm was still in the way of the wheel. He jerked it down in her lap. "Stay the hell out of the way of the yoke!" he said.

Player was taxiing, going to the other end of the field to turn and make his takeoff into the wind. He said, "I hope you noticed we're in a 152."

"Yeah, yeah, yeah. I know."

"We didn't lose that much gas."

"No shit. I have blind faith in your talent, though. Now just get this mother off the ground."

Player turned back into the wind and gunned the engine up until the rpm needle was almost at the red line. He said, "I hope you know what we're doing."

"Me? Hell, you're flying the goddam airplane."

Claudie said, her face against his ear, "Oh, I don't know how to—"

He put his hand over her mouth. "Shut up! We ain't gone yet. And keep your body away from that wheel! You interfere with that and we're in trouble."

Player was standing on the toe brakes, the engine at full rev. China could feel it surging against the restraint of the brakes. Player looked over at him. "Anything you want to tell me before it's too late?"

"No."

"Who was the old man?"

"Her husband."

"Oh," Player said. "Well, that explains it. Now we're kidnapping wives." He suddenly released the toe brakes and the airplane began to lurch forward. It moved slowly, straining to pick up speed. They bounced over the rough ground, gradually moving faster and faster. Cocking his head to one side to see past the girl's head, China could see the air-speed indicator on the instrument panel. The needle was bouncing around forty mph. Normally you could get a 152 off at fifty knots. But he figured, as loaded as they were, they were going to need around seventy.

The plane was moving faster, skimming the ground with its wheels now. But Player held the wheel forward, keeping the airplane on the ground while the speed built. Ahead of them the ground rose to a little ridge topped by a line of trees. It had been a good way off at first, but now it was coming closer and closer. Player held the nose down until they ran out of the green pasture. Then he gentled the wheel back and they were off the ground and flying. They cleared the ridge with a good ten feet to spare, but they needed to gain at least a thousand feet to clear the low mountains back to the northeast and directly in their flight path.

China said, "You better circle around in this valley and get some altitude."

"Yeah," Player said, concentrating on flying the airplane. He let off fifteen degrees of flaps and the airplane became less sluggish. They began to circle slowly in the little valley, clawing upward for altitude. Player said, "This son-of-a-bitch is flying right on the thin edge of stall. Don't anybody make any sudden moves."

From behind the girl China watched the altimeter creep up slowly. They had a hundred feet above the ground, then two hundred and then three. But they were going to need a thousand to clear the high ground.

They continued to circle. Player said, "You have anything to say about this?" Without taking his eyes from the instruments, he nodded his head sideways at the girl.

"Not now," China said. "Later. You just get this son-of-a-bitch up to altitude."

Player glanced out the window on his side. They were circling almost directly over the signal fire. Player said, "I believe husband has retrieved his shotgun. In fact I think husband is going to take a shot at us."

China glanced at the altimeter. They had almost five hundred feet. He said, "He can't hit us at this altitude with a shotgun."

"No," Player said. "But I imagine he's going to work off an awful lot of frustration in the attempt. I know I would if someone had just stolen my wife."

China said, "It ain't like it seems."

"It never is. Does Bonnie know about this? Or should I say, does Bonnie approve?"

"Goddammit, will you just hold up until we get to Laredo? You can do that, can't you? Or are you just going to flap your jaw about this for the next hour?"

"I'll say no more," Player said. "Not another word. Except I wonder if Bonnie would have been so frantic for me to come down here and rescue your cornbread ass if she'd known what you were bringing home. But I guess you'll explain this lady as the new cleaning girl. Is that the drift?"

"Player, I'm warning you."

"Not another word. This lady isn't a Mormon, is she?"

"Player, are you going to take us down in flames with your yak-yak-yak or are you going to pay attention and get us out of here?"

"I ain't passing no judgments. I want that clear. Far be

it for me to say a word. But I will point out that from where I'm sitting this lady ain't wearing no underwear."

"Goddammit!" China said. Claudie had her legs tucked up in his lap, against her chest. Her dress had ridden up around her waist. China tried to pull it down, but their position was too constricted. "Goddam you, Player. You son-of-a-bitch. I got enough trouble."

"I say not a word," Player said. "Some night, when you and me and Bonnie and Jane are all sitting around having a drink after dinner, I will not mention that you spent a couple of days with a very good-looking young lady who doesn't wear underwear."

"Oh shit!" China said. "If you knew—" Then he stopped. "Just get us to Laredo."

They had seven hundred feet and Player turned on heading, still climbing. They topped the low mountains and then the land fell away, lowering as they headed for the border.

China and Player did not talk much because of the girl. They had plenty to say to each other, but it could wait. The plane was flying all right now, slowly and heavily, but with a margin for error. The girl, who'd seemed so light when she'd first climbed on top of him, now seemed, to weigh a ton. He said to her, "For a soft looking girl you've got the sharpest goddam hipbone I've ever felt." His left leg was numb from the thigh down.

She tried to shift, but he told her, "No, don't move. Just take it easy."

But finally he pushed her up to where she was sitting on his left knee. He said, "Keep your feet away from the rudder pedals and your hands clear of that wheel."

She had been good and not said a word. But now she looked around at him. "Thanks," she said. "You went out of your way."

"Forget it," he said.

He noticed that Player kept rubbing the back of his neck. He said, "What the hell's the matter with you? Got a crick?"

"I don't know," Player said. He ran his hand over his neck and then under his jaw. "Seems kind of sore, kind of swollen. Guess I slept the wrong way on the pillow last night. Just a little stiff."

"You can fly the airplane, can't you?"

Player looked over at him, that sardonic grin taking over his face. "What the hell does it look like I'm doing? Besides, would I fail in front of the master and his lady?"

An hour later they were making their final approach into Laredo. Player landed smoothly and then taxied toward the parking area. A line boy came out from the flying service station headquarters and directed them to a parking place. China saw that it was Kenny. But then Player was killing the engine. China frantically opened the door and manhandled the girl across his body and shoved her out the door. For a moment he leaned his head back and shut his eyes, savoring the sudden release of her weight. He climbed out of the airplane slowly, both legs still a little numb, and stamped his feet on the concrete for a moment to get the circulation going. Then he retrieved his bags.

By the time he walked away from the airplane, Player and the girl were already waiting for him fifteen yards away. Kenny came around from the front of the airplane. "Mister Blue," he said, "what the hell?"

China said, "Tend to the airplane, Kenny. And then come and drive me and my friend to the motel."

He walked off, leaving the line boy staring after him.

Player said, "Once again I've saved your ass. How many times does this make?"

"Cut the shit," China said. "You got plenty of money?"

"Yeah, sure."

"Give me two hundred."

Player got out his billfold and handed China two one-hundred-dollar bills. He took them and turned to the girl. "Here," he said. "Take this."

She looked at the money and then up to his face. "I don't need any more."

"Yeah, you do," he said. He stuffed it into the waist of her skirt. He said, "Now look, we're split. I got business and you got business. I got you here and you've got money to get you somewhere else. Fair?"

She suddenly put her arms around his neck and kissed him on the mouth. When she pulled back, she said, "You really are a classy guy." Then she turned and went walking off.

Player was looking at him with that little cynical grin. China said, "Don't say a goddam word. Let's go to the motel. I want to get these goddam clothes off me and take a shower."

Kenny drove them back to the motel. When they got out of the pickup, China handed the boy a twenty-dollar bill. "Here," he said, "go buy yourself another flying lesson."

"Mister Blue," the boy said, "what happened? How come you didn't come back in the airplane you left in? Did something go wrong?"

China said, with a touch of grimness in his voice, "Son, if I was to tell you, it'd turn you right off of your chosen career. Just live in ignorance and grow up to be an airline pilot."

They got in the room and China had a long, cool shower. He came out of the bathroom, drying off. Player was slumped on one of the beds, rubbing the back of his neck.

China said, "You're doing it again. What the hell's the matter with you? Are you sick?"

Player laughed and shook his head. "Naw, reckon not."

Then he put his hand down to his throat. "Must be catching a cold or something. I think I'm getting a sore throat."

"Hell, let's have a drink. That'll fix you up." He took the bottle of cheap Mexican brandy out of his flight kit and poured them both a stiff shot and then watered it down a little with tap water. They toasted in the manner of pilots. Player said, "No surprise landings," and China said, "VFR all the way. Severely clear."

Player took a drink and made a face. "Where'd you get the whiskey, from a veterinarian?"

"No, that whiskey was picked out for me by my latest benefactor. The husband of the lady we kidnapped."

Player said, "I figure he paid you back in spades. Jesus, I don't know if you're supposed to drink this stuff or thin paint with it."

China got up off the bed where he'd been sitting and began gathering up a fresh pair of jeans and a shirt. He said, "I got to get dressed and go tell Gomez the bad news about his airplane and cargo. I don't think he's going to be happy."

"Probably not," Player said. "But then you can't win them all."

While he put on clean clothes China told Player about what had happened. When he was finished, the other pilot shrugged and said, "Well, that's life in the fast lane. So you figure somebody leaked?"

"Hell, yes!" China said. "Those goddam *Federales* weren't there because they're clairvoyant. They knew where and when I was arriving, and they had enough of a welcome party arranged to capture a half a dozen smugglers. The only reason I ain't dead or sitting in a Mexican jail right now is because I didn't kill the engines and I didn't get out of the airplane."

"You think it was that clerk of Gomez's?"

"Who else could it have been? He was out of the plane

and gone before the shooting started. I bet he's got himself a nice reward and is sitting up there in Monterey or some place right now wishing they'd of shot me down so the payoff could have been even bigger. Being as how I left with that goddam starboard engine out, they probably think I crashed and burned anyway. It's a goddam miracle I didn't.''

He sat down on the bed to pull on his boots. Player had lain back; he was rubbing his neck again. China said, ''So as far as I'm concerned, we cross Mister Gomez off our list. His money is nice, but he's not protecting us from the risks involved. It was his clerk this time. Next time it'll be somebody else. I'm going to so advise the man in New York. You other crazy people can do what you want, but I've made my last run for him.''

Player said, ''You're probably right.'' He was lying back on the bed. He yawned and rubbed his neck just under his cheek bones. He seemed very lethargic.

China said, ''Say, are you all right? What's the matter?''

''Naw, I'm fine,'' Player said. He passed a hand over his forehead. ''Just seems a little hot in here. I guess it was that brandy.''

''Hot?'' China looked at him. ''Hell, man, the air conditioner is going full blast. It's cold as a witch's tit.''

''If you say so,'' Player said listlessly. ''Listen, go lay the good news on Gomez and then let's get the hell out of here. I've got to leave for Puerto Rico tomorrow. I keep forgetting I got a job to do on my own. Spend all my time dragging your ass out of trouble.''

''Well, listen, I'll be back quick and then we'll go out for some dinner. Maybe you ought to catch a nap or something.''

''Or something,'' Player said. He laid his head back on the pillow. Then he raised it up as China started for the door. ''Just one question,'' he said. ''Am I really supposed to believe you turned down a piece of ass off that lady with no underwear? I mean, are you putting that out as a serious, believable piece of news?''

"Yeah," China said. "I told it to you straight. I turned it down. And for the reason I told you."

Player said dryly, "That is un-fucking-believable. And I mean that literally. I had a pretty basic look at that non-underwear wearing lady and she doesn't look that cullable. Have you finally, as I've been predicting for years, turned queer? I mean, I'm grooved into the old married routine on account of Lady Jane, but you still proclaim yourself available for private parties and out-of-town appearances. What the hell was wrong?''

China smiled slightly and shook his head. "Like I told you, Player, I just didn't like her style."

Player shook his head and grinned his sardonic grin. "Well, won't Miss Bonnie be pleased. I can't wait to tell her. Unless you are lying to a hero. Do you give me your word as my worst enemy that you didn't ravish that extremely assailable young woman?''

"I wouldn't have fucked her with your dick," China said.

Player laid his head back on the pillow. "Then the only thing I can tell you, buddy," he said, "is that you're shopping without a grocery list. Go on and get out of here. I've known you past your point of no return."

China shook his head and went out of the motel. In the cab on his way to Gomez's office, he thought of how good it was going to be to take a rest. He'd been going too hard for too long a time. He was getting stale, slowing up just that half-second that could sometimes mean the difference. He needed about two weeks out of action. Player would get his assignment over with and then they'd go off and do some crazy stuff, get the batteries recharged, have a little fun, get a little drunk, maybe hunt and fish a little.

At the warehouse another clerk, a young one, was behind the desk where Pepe had been. China pointed at the door to Gomez's office. "He in?"

The young clerk said, "Yes, I will tell him you wish to see him if you will give me your name."

"Never mind," China said. "He's expecting me."

He pushed the door open and went in. Gomez was sitting behind his desk, looking over some papers and smoking a cigar. He looked up as China came in. "Ah, my friend," he said. "*Bienevedos.*"

"Fuck your welcome," China said. He went over to the refrigerator in the corner, got out a cold beer, and then slumped down in the padded chair across from Gomez. He looked at the fat man for a long second and then said, "They were waiting for me when I got there."

Gomez raised his hands and sighed. "I heard. My brother-in-law called me on the telephone. Very unfortunate. I wonder how they knew?"

"Bullshit," China said. "I would imagine you're surprised to see me. I'm supposed to be dead in the wreck of that crate you had me fly. Or didn't brother-in-law bother to mention they were shooting at me?"

Gomez took a handkerchief out of his pocket and wiped his face. The office was as hot as ever. "Yes," he said, "he told me that the police were over-zealous. Damned unfortunate."

China took a long drink of beer. Then he said, "Gomez, you say once more that my nearly getting my ass shot off was very unfortunate and I'm going to come over that desk and finish what nature started—by cramming your fat head completely inside your fat body. There was nothing unfortunate about it. Your goddam fucking Pepe sold the information to the police. I've thought about it long and hard and it's the only explanation that adds up."

Gomez looked down at his desk. Then he picked his

cigar out of the ash tray and took a puff. "I believe you are right," he said.

China said, "Hah! Believe, shit! Somebody drew them a map and that somebody was right here in this office. I don't figure it was you, so it had to be your boy, Pepe. Well, you've fucked me over for the last time. This goddam job is dangerous enough as it is without any help from the people at this end. So, sport, you just forget the phone number of the man in New York. So far as I'm concerned, you've had it, Gomez. You ain't trustworthy. And that's the way the report goes back."

Gomez said, "Now wait, amigo. Don't be unreasonable about this." He got out his handkerchief again and wiped at his face. He suddenly looked very disturbed. "Look, I've lost the airplane, which was worth many thousands of dollars. And I've lost the cargo, also worth many thousands of dollars. The only way I have to recoup my losses is to export more goods. You can see that. I'm a businessman and so are you. Be reasonable."

"Go to hell, Gomez," China said. "I'm not a businessman. Business men sit behind their safe desks and don't take any risks for all the money they make. As for your cargo and your airplane . . ." He got out of the chair, took a pencil off of Gomez's desk, went to the map and made a mark where he'd crash-landed the DC-3. He said, "There's your goddam airplane, Jack. And all your electronic cargo. Of course, there's a man there who has probably sold it by now, but you ought to be able to get some of it back." He turned around and looked at Gomez, taking a second to light a cigarette. He said, "It ain't lost. None of it. It's just stored in an out-of-the-way place. And you know as well as I do that you can go and get it or go and buy it back from the Mexican police. You ain't lost nothing except a little of your profit. So let's don't kid each other. I damn near got my ass shot off, which I don't exactly cotton to.

Plus, I am considerably bruised up from landing that crate you gave me to fly. And that's not to mention the loss of my time and my fee.''

Gomez tapped the ash off his cigar in the tray. "About that," he said, "what if I were to give you, say, a third of your fee? Just between you and me. Not send it to New York. How would that sound to you? Would that smooth over our little problem?''

"Go to hell, Gomez," China repeated.

"How about half? Half your fee? Or maybe just a straight three thousand dollars. That's better than half. Maybe you'd want to forget about this.''

"I told you to go to hell," China said. "If you don't understand the English language, maybe I can get an interpreter in here.''

"Say, amigo, have a heart. I got to make some more loads. I need your organization.''

China dropped his cigarette on the floor and ground it out with his boot. He said, "Now listen to me carefully, fat man. That wasn't just a little leak, it was a big leak. There were so goddam many soldiers around that landing strip they looked like they'd been *camped* out there. I will take my lumps on the fee. But if you think I'd risk my neck again, or allow any of my brother pilots to walk into this kind of a loaded-dice situation again, you are out of your fucking mind. You have gotten too fucking undependable and you are through with our outfit. I ain't going to get any of my buddies killed.''

He turned around and walked out of the office, with Gomez protesting behind him. He was angry, but there wasn't much he could do about his anger except let it slowly wear off. Maybe Gomez wasn't responsible for what his clerk had done, but in this line of work you couldn't afford to give anybody the benefit of the doubt.

When he got back to the motel, Player was still lying on

the bed, resting his head on the pillow. Even in the dim of the room his face looked flushed. He opened his eyes as China came in. "Hey, cowboy," he said.

China looked at him sharply. His voice had sounded very weak. "What the hell's the matter with you? You going to stay in that bed all day? I thought you had to go to Puerto Rico."

Player shook his head. "Don't know what's the matter with me. Feel a little funny. Maybe it was that cheap brandy you forced on me."

"Yeah?" China said. "Then how come I ain't sick?" He went over to the bed and felt his friend's forehead. He was burning hot. China said, "Buddy, I don't know what you got, but you got something."

"Maybe just a little sore throat." He put his hand up and rubbed just below his jaw. "Feels kind of swollen."

China said, "We got to call a doctor. We got to check this out." He reached for the phone.

Player said, "Hey, cowboy, forget that. I don't need a doctor. I'll be all right in a minute. I got an assignment, don't forget."

"Fuck it," China said. "Listen, it sounds like you've got some kind of an upper respiratory ailment and pilots do not fuck with upper respiratory ailments. Tends to mess up the old middle ear, buddy. And if that gets screwed up, you're out of business. I'm calling a doctor."

With Player protesting all the while, he called the desk and asked them to send a doctor around as soon as possible. The desk clerk said, "Mister, I don't think a doctor will come. They don't make house calls, I don't think."

China said, "You find one. We don't make calls on doctors' offices. Tell him we pay cash, and plenty of it."

When he was off the phone, Player looked at him and shook his head. "We are going to be a trifle embarrassed when the doctor comes all this way to tell me I've got a sore throat. Blue, how come you have always got to do things contrary to accepted practices?''

"I was born contrary," China said. He lit a cigarette. "You just lie there and shut up."

"Man, look, I got an assignment. It's got to get done. Surely even you can understand that."

But he said it without much force. He looked sick and acted sick.

China sat there watching him until the phone rang. It was the desk. The clerk said, "Listen, Mister, I called the emergency room of the hospital. They said your friend should come there."

China said, "Fuck that. Tell them I have the foreign diplomat for a very important South American country here and he cannot be moved. Tell them to send a doctor. Tell them it's a matter of internal security."

From his bed Player laughed weakly. "Boy, you are the cat's pajamas. Why don't we just make a little run over to the emergency room? Save some trouble."

"Hell, no," China said. "We make plenty of money by risking our ass. Let's enjoy the fruit of that ass-risking by making the doctor come to us. We are not cattle, my man; we do not sit in emergency waiting rooms."

Player laughed weakly. "Cowboy," he said, "you are truly one of the heroes of this or any other generation. I have just now recognized you. You are really Hopalong Cassidy who I used to see at the cowboy movies on Saturday mornings at the Franklin Theatre in good old Temple, Texas."

"Keep it to yourself," China said. "By the way, do you really have plenty of cash? I only have about five hundred left. I can get some more depending on how extensive your medical treatment is going to be."

Player shook his head, rolling it slowly from side to side on the pillow. "Got plenty. Got a little better than two grand. Didn't know how much I'd need on the Puerto Rico run. In case I up and die, it's in my billfold.''

The phone rang. China answered it. The desk clerk said, ''Well, mister, they say they'll send a doctor over. They say it'll have to be cash. Is your friend really a foreign diplomat from a South American country?''

''Yes,'' China said. ''He's the Minister of Didactic Linguistics. Very important. Tell the doctor to hurry.'' He hung up.

''What the hell does that mean?'' Player asked. ''What you said.''

China leaned back on the bed and yawned. ''I don't know. But if it works, who cares?''

After a minute he got out of his chair and poured himself a glass of brandy and water. He said, ''You don't look like you want any of this.''

''You got that right,'' Player said. ''Incredible how quick on the draw you are.'' He put his hand up to his brow. Then he said, ''Shit! Am I getting sick? I mean really getting sick? I can't afford to get sick. I got an assignment.''

China said, ''Son, bacteria do not respect professions. In fact they will even go so far as to cross a picket line. I wish that doctor would get here. You're starting to look pretty bad and I damn sure don't want any stiffs on my hands.'' He took a drink of the brandy and water and made a face. He said, ''Why am I drinking this shit? Why didn't I get something a little better the minute I hit civilization?''

Player said, ''Because you are a dumb ex-rodeo cowboy and don't have any sense. You have fallen on your head too many times.''

His voice sounded weak and thin. To China he was looking increasingly bad. China said, ''Look, hombre, if you are going to get sick, I wish you'd do a good job of it. Frankly, I wish you'd die. I'm tired of your face, which

looks exactly like a horned toad's. You are probably one
of the ugliest human beings I've ever seen.''

Player coughed slightly and sighed. "Just like you,
Blue. Pick on me when I'm down. You wouldn't dare talk
to me like that if I was in fettle. You know, one of these
days you are going to get so bold as to hit me and I'm
going to find out about it later and then your ass is in big
trouble.''

"Listen, Howard," China said, "which I happen to
know is your real name—and which, if you ain't careful,
I'm going to spread around—if I ever hit you, you will
only find out about it as you come out of the anesthetic
administered to you during the brain operation necessitated
by the severe subdural hematoma I will have inflicted on
you.''

Player laughed weakly. "Blue, if I live through this,
I'm going to have you killed. I've already figured out how
I'm going to do it. I'm going to have you turned loose on a
school playground and have two third-graders beat you to
death. Shouldn't take more than three or four minutes.''

China lit a cigarette. "Listen," he said, "die slowly and
painfully, will you? You know I'm an Indian and I never
forget. I have been waiting to pay you back for a long
time. You remember about fifteen years ago? When we
were still rodeoing and we were in Baton Rouge and I had
that luscious little shiny bright who could not wait to mate
with me? And you got the key to my motel room and
slipped in there and mayonnaised the sheets, thereby cost-
ing me what might have been a world class piece of ass?
Because that young lady just took a shower and put on her
clothes and left? Leaving me in a very erect position, and
in a lot of pain and suffering from unfulfilled expectations?
Have you forgotten that?''

Player laughed a little. "No, nor have I forgotten the
time you fixed me up with that drag queen and I didn't

figure out what the fuck was going on until the queer-assed bastard got his panties off. Blue, one of these days I'll fix you for that one. Man, you are evil.''

China leaned forward in his chair and looked at his friend. He said, "What the fuck you figure you got?"

Player shook his head slowly. "Don't know."

"Were you feeling bad when you left home?"

"Not that bad. I just thought maybe I was getting a sore throat. Listen, hadn't you better call Bonnie and let her know you got out all right? She was about semi-hysterical when she called me last night.''

China said, "I will when I know what the deal is on you. I'm liable to have to sit down here and hold your hand. How'd you come, by the way? In your 310?"

"Yeah," Player said. "Then I rented that 152 out at the airport."

"You close it out?"

"It's paid for," Player said. "And reported in. I did that while you were kissing Miss No Underwear good-bye."

There was a knock at the door. China answered it to find a small man of Mexican extraction carrying a little black bag standing there. He said, "I am Doctor Herrera. Is someone sick here?"

"Come in, Doc" China said. "We have a *very* sick man here. However, he's on a delicate mission for the embassy, so you've got to keep this under you hat.''

The doctor glanced at him and came into the room. He had slicked-back hair and a pencil mustache. He did not look amused. He gestured at Player. "Is this the patient?"

"Yeah," China said. "Such as he is."

The doctor sat down on Player's bed and began the examination. He looked into Player's mouth and ears and nasal passages and eyes. He felt under the pilot's jawbones. Then he put his instruments away and closed his bag. He stood up. He said, "Your friend has the mumps. He must go to the hospital."

"He's got what?"

"He has the mumps. I do not see why you have dragged me out here to this motel. I am the chief internist at the hospital. You could have brought him there. He must go immediately, right now." He was a very severe-looking young man with no humor in his face.

China said, "But the mumps! Hell, that's a kid's disease."

The doctor said, "Be that as it may, there is no doubt about this diagnosis. He must be hospitalized. Mumps in a man of his age can have serious consequences if they are not treated properly. Will you take him to the hospital or will I call for an ambulance?"

Player said weakly, "China. The assignment. I got to figure that out."

"Yeah," China said, thinking rapidly. "Yeah, I know what you mean." He turned to the doctor. "I'll have him there within an hour. But first he and I have got to have a little talk."

The doctor looked at him dubiously. "I warn you," he said, "that mumps in an adult male can be serious. All I can do for him here is call for the ambulance. In any case, you owe me fifty dollars."

China stood up and got out his billfold. He did not like the way the severe young doctor was looking at him, or talking at him. He got out a hundred-dollar bill and folded it and shoved it in the doctor's breast pocket. He said, "Listen, *chumacho*," which was not a term of endearment except among Spanish friends of long standing, "spare us your I'm-the-doctor God Almighty bullshit. I will tell it to you in sequence. First of all, my friend and I have to conduct a little business before he can go to the hospital. So we don't want an ambulance. Secondly, go buy yourself a bedside manner with the change from that hundred.

Thirdly, my friend will be at your hospital in half an hour and he will want a private room and the best possible treatment. And lastly," spat China as he reached out and took the little doctor by the collar and raised him up to his tiptoes, "if he *doesn't* get the best possible treatment, if anything goes wrong with him, I will come back here and cut your heart out and burn your hospital down. Now, get your ass out of here and get back to that hospital and tell them to get ready for a very special patient."

The doctor stood there staring at him.

China made little pushing motions with his hands. "Shoo, shoo," he said. "Go on, boy. Shoo."

After the doctor had turned and rushed out of the room, Player put his hand to his forehead and laughed weakly. "Oh shit, Blue," he said. "Thanks a lot. They'll probably strangle me in my sleep at that hospital after your help. Man, you are never going to win any diplomatic awards."

"Fuck that shit," China said. He sat down. "Am I thinking what you're thinking?"

"Yeah," Player said. "Tag, you're it. Puerto Rico, here you come."

"Oh fuck!" China said. He leaned back in his chair and put his hand over his eyes. Then he turned to Player. "The mumps! A goddam kid's disease! This is a hell of a trick to play on an orphan. Listen, man, I'm tired. I want to go home! I don't want your fucking assignment."

Player said, "You better call the man. And then get me to a hospital. I'm near death."

China said, "You are the worst enemy any human being ever had." But he swiveled around in his chair and picked up the phone and put in a call to the man in New York.

The man in New York was always at home. He'd been immobilized from the waist down twenty-five years ago in a flying accident, and now he sat in his penthouse apartment in a wheelchair where he was attended by a cook and a valet. China had met him once in person. Beneath the layers of age that inactivity had put on the man, China had been able to see the man that had once been a very daring, very resourceful pilot. The physical strength was gone, but the emotional strength was still there.

The phone was answered. The man said, "Yes?"

"China. The Mexico run was a washout for reasons I'll explain later. Cancel Gomez. He's gotten too dangerous. He leaks. Or people in his operation leak."

"Very well," the man said. "Next?"

"Player is down. He's sick. He's going to be in a hospital here in Laredo. I'm going to need what cash he's got on him. Get a bunch of money down to him. In a hurry. And make sure he gets well taken care of."

"That's done. What else?"

China sighed. "I guess I'll take his assignment. Anything I need to know outside of what he can tell me?"

There was a silence for a moment, and then the man said, "No, not really. However, these are first-time clients and I'd be extremely careful with them. Their references were a little shaky. But then, that's been the case before. Only don't trust them for anything. The total fee is twelve thousand and you should collect half of that before you go wheels up. Get six thousand dollars and put it in a safe place, not on your person, before you take off. These people are South Americans and I don't trust them entirely."

China said; "If you don't trust them, why in the fuck are we taking the assignment?"

The man said coldly, "Risks go with the territory. Or haven't you heard?"

China said, "Oh, fuck you. I hope the tires go flat on your wheelchair."

He hung up the phone and lit a cigarette and looked at Player. He said, "Well, this is another fine mess you've gotten me into, Ollie."

Player laughed. He sounded feverish. He said, "Actually, it's all a gag. As soon as you head out for Puerto Rico, I'm taking off for your house to see Bonnie. We've been planning this for years."

China drew on his cigarette. "I don't doubt it. I've heard some strange stories from ladies that we've had in common. One told me you got your kicks by licking wet polish off her toe nails."

"Yeah," Player sighed. "That acetone will get you every time." He started to say something else and then coughed and closed his eyes.

China stubbed his cigarette out in the ashtray. He said, "I guess we better get your ass to the hospital." He picked up the phone and called the flight service station and asked for Kenny. When the boy came on the line, sounding breathless, China said, "Get over here, Kenny. I got a passenger for the hospital. My partner. Hurry. And don't let your boss say you can't come."

The boy said, "Yessir, Mister Blue! I'm on my way."

China said to Player, "Okay, ace, tell me as much about this trick as you can."

He listened while Player went over the details. When his friend was finished, China frowned slightly. He said, "Then I've got to be there tomorrow. I won't take your 310. I'll leave that for you in case you get out of the hospital before I get back. I'll take a commercial down to Miami Beach and then rent something there. What do you recommend I get?"

Player said, sounding weaker and weaker, "A twin engine. There's four people besides you, so you'd better just rent another 310."

"Yeah," China said. He yawned and rubbed his hand over his face. "I'll call the airlines in a minute. Shit, I'm tired. All I really want to do is go home and cuddle up to Miss Bonnie." He shook his head. "Howard," he said, "why do I allow you to keep on doing this to me? You have been putting hardships on me for a long, long time. Why do I allow it?"

"I told you," Player said, "you're a dumb ass."

"But the big question," China said, leaning back, "is why are four people from South America willing to pay twelve thousand dollars to get flown from Puerto Rico to somewhere down South and back again? Illegal aliens come into the country every day for a hell of a lot less money than that. What's their angle?"

Player lifted a weak arm off the bed and pointed a finger toward the ceiling. "Ah," he said, "there's the real question. And the only real answer to that is that we get paid a lot of money for not asking questions." Then he turned his head slowly and looked at China. "But if I was you, cowboy, I'd be damn careful to watch my ass. Something tells me that these are people that not even a nasty fuck like you would want to tangle with."

Chapter Six

Later that evening he caught a connecting flight out of Laredo for Miami. It was going to be a long night of traveling, but with any luck he'd be in Puerto Rico in time for the appointment with his clients.

It got dark not too long after the plane lifted off and he settled back in his seat and closed his eyes. More than a little drunk, he was truly tired and he missed Bonnie. He'd been looking forward to going home and he hadn't wanted to take over Player's assignment.

But there hadn't been any help for it. The man in New York couldn't have rerouted another pilot in time—not with any guarantee that the whole assignment wouldn't be blown all to hell by the time someone three times removed from the situation had been hastily briefed on all the details.

So he'd really had no choice. But he sat there in the seat promising himself, faithfully, that when this job was over,

118

he was going to take a rest—a long rest. Bonnie was right; he had too much money in the bank to push himself the way he did. For a little over five years he'd been making close to a quarter of a million dollars a year. Everything he owned was paid for. He didn't owe anyone a cent. And he had over two hundred thousand dollars in the bank, drawing interest. He could retire tomorrow and never have to worry about money again.

Player had been plenty sick when Kenny had come by to take him to the hospital. He'd even been too sick to joke. China had said, "If I were you, buddy, I wouldn't start any continued stories. Or make any plans much beyond tomorrow."

Player had just grinned weakly while they were helping him out to Kenny's pickup. Then he'd sat there slumped in his seat, his head on his chest. He'd really looked sick and China had almost felt like sympathizing with him. But instead he'd said, "Well, I'm in luck. Your wife told me she wants another kid and if you'll stay in the hospital just a day longer than it takes me to get back from Puerto Rico, I'll be able to help her out. She's told me about your little problem."

Player had said, "Go fuck yourself," but he'd said it weakly.

Well, he'd be all right. Player had survived much worse with hardly a blink of an eye and the man from New York would be checking on him to make sure he was getting the best treatment.

It was a tiring trip. He had to change planes in Dallas and then again in Atlanta, so he didn't get to Miami until three in the morning. He was so tired and starved for sleep that he just checked into an airport hotel, left a wake-up call, and then tumbled into bed and went straight to sleep.

Still feeling like hell, he was up by eight o'clock. He took a hot shower, shaved and dressed, and was in a cab an hour later, on his way to a flying service at a little airport in Miami Beach. He'd often left from Miami Beach for runs down to Cuba and other places, and through the years he and the owner of the service, a man in his early fifties named Cliff Finch, had become friends. He was an old pilot who'd spent his whole life in aviation, though he'd mostly retired to the business sideline in his later years. He knew what China did.

At the little airport China paid off his cab and entered the small frame building where Finch's offices were located. The owner was leaning over the counter cleaning his teeth when China came through the door carrying his bags. He groaned and looked away when he saw China. "Oh no," he said, "Oh no! Not today, lord, not today!" Then he looked at China. He said, "Just turn around and go back to wherever you came from if you're here for what I think you're here for. I don't need any airplanes shot up today, thank you."

China sat his bags down and went to the counter. He got out a cigarette and lit it. "Finch," he said, "it only happened once. And it happened in an airplane that I rented from you and that should have had a major overhaul about a hundred hours back. That thing didn't have enough power to take off downhill. And besides that, there were damn few bullet holes in the airplane. And I should have reported you to the FAA for exceeding annual requirements on the engine as it was." He put out his hand. "How you doing, ugly?"

Finch shook. He had a hard, square hand. He was balding and running a little to fat, but there was still the frame of a powerful man under the extra pounds. He said; "Hell, China, I was just thinking about you the other day when the weather advisory put out a hurricane warning. And here you are. Don't tell me where you're going or why; just tell me what chance I have of getting my airplane back."

"Two chances. Slim and none." China leaned up against the counter. "Need a twin. You got a 310?"

Finch shook his head. "No. Got a Piper Apache."

"IFR bird?"

Finch raised his eyebrows. "Would I offer you anything else, knowing that you will try to find the worst possible weather?"

"I'd rather have the Apache. Does better on short fields. Best I can figure, I'll need it for two or three days."

Finch pushed away from the counter. "I'll tell the hired hands to get it ready." He turned back. "You had breakfast? Or are you in too big of a rush as usual?"

China said, "If you're buying, I got plenty of time."

"Then just let me tell the line crew to kiss the Apache good-bye. We'll probably never see it again."

A little later Finch drove them down to a cafe not far from the airport. After the waitress had taken their order, the flight station operator asked, "Where's that running buddy of yours, Player? He doing all right?"

China told him what had happened. He said, "I got to laugh, though it ain't real funny."

"The mumps. Ain't they supposed to hit a grown man in the balls? Make him sterile? Or is that the measles?"

"I don't know," China said. "Either way, he's got enough kids." Then he told Finch about how Player had picked him up in Mexico. "Little son-of-a-bitch saved my ass. That's all I know."

Finch turned his head, a look in his eyes. Then he said, sighing, "I don't know, maybe it's just because I'm getting old. But I envy you guys. I wish maybe I'd gotten the chance to do the kind of flying you guys are doing. It sounds like what a pilot *ought* to be doing—flying the way those guys back in World War One used to fly. Know what I mean?''

China smiled slightly. "The old Hat-in-the-Ring squadron. Yeah, I know what you mean." Now he looked away. "Maybe that's the reason we do it."

Just then the waitress brought their eggs and bacon. She kept trying to put coffee in China's empty cup. He put his hand over it, motioning at the Coke she'd brought him. When she was gone, he said, "Now, God save me from being the robot she thinks I am. Why the goddam hell do people expect you to be so fucking predictable? She hasn't got sense enough to note that I don't drink coffee. It ain't her pushing the coffee that burns my ass. It's the fact that she expects me to be like everybody else. *That's* what pisses me off."

Finch regarded him for a moment. He said, "You're wound kind of tight this morning, little brother. Is this little sortie you're fixing to take off on going to be a rough one?"

China motioned with his fork and shrugged. "I don't know. I guess I'm just tired. It's kind of off the beaten track, I know that."

He thought about what he and Player had talked about, before his friend had gotten so sick he'd had trouble communicating. Player had warned him, "Now, cowboy, remember, the man in New York doesn't know a whole hell of a lot about these pilgrims. They are not regular customers."

China had said, "No solid line on them at all?"

"Oh," Player had said, "they knew some of the right names to drop. But the man still thinks there's something funny. They're just willing to pay too damn much money for a relatively easy job. And they won't specify destination other than to say it's somewhere in the southern U.S. and they won't say how long they'll need you except it won't be more than two or three days. So you make damn sure you get half that fee before you even let them see the insides of the airplane."

China didn't think they sounded all that different from a lot of other new and unproven clients he'd heard about. More than one customer had agreed to a big price simply because they'd had no intention of paying it. They'd just point a gun at the pilot's head once they got airborne, and force him to fly them wherever they wanted to go.

So they'd taken a few precautionary measures to make sure such practices didn't become routine.

And Player had said, "So the man is worried about the no destination and the no specific time limit. He's not sure, of course, but he doubts their front as political refugees. He thinks they are running from a little more than bad luck at the polls in some banana republic. He doesn't know exactly what it is, but he told me to watch myself. I give you the same good advice."

China regarded Finch. "It'll probably be a milk run. Really, I think I just need a rest."

Finch said, "By the way, how come you drink Cokes in the morning? That don't even seem American. Might even be communistic."

China said, "Because I *like* Cokes in the morning. How does that hit you, motherfucker!"

They both laughed. Finch said, "Well, little brother, I sure hope you *and* my airplane get back here safe."

"I'll only vouch for myself," China said.

An hour later he was wheels up and climbing through the low cumulus clouds on a heading for Puerto Rico, roughly two hundred fifty miles away. He had an appointment at noon with his passengers at a cafe in the little town of Fujardo, on the eastern coast of the island.

It took him almost an hour and a half to make the flight because of the build-up of a developing weather front. The cumulus clouds, as they picked up heat from the rising sun, were rapidly turning into thunderheads. China had his hands full staying out of turbulence and trouble. It was a good thing he'd gotten off as early as he had. By midafternoon the front would be fully developed and flying between Puerto Rico and the mainland would be difficult and dangerous in a small plane that was incapable of getting to the twenty-five and thirty-thousand-foot altitudes necessary to top the thunderheads.

The Piper Apache he'd rented from Cliff Finch was a good, dependable twin-engine airplane of no particularly spectacular performance capability. It could carry six people and could fly fairly well with one engine out, though it was best that that engine did not go out on takeoff or at too low an altitude since the airplane required some trimming and adjusting before it would limp along on one fan. What China liked about it best was that for a plane in its class it had good short field takeoff and landing capabilities. And that, on the kind of job he half expected he'd be facing, could be very important.

Homing in on the VOR station near San Juan, he had no trouble finding the little town of Fujardo. The airport there was noncontrolled and very small. Therefore, China just signalled his intentions to the pilots in his area on the air-to-air frequency, set up his pattern and landed. No line boy came out to guide him to a parking place, so he just taxied into a line of planes on the grass apron beside the runway, killed his engines and unloaded the airplane. He noticed that even though the airport was very tiny, there were a good number of private planes, both single and multi-engine, tied down on the grass sward. Fujardo, he knew, was an important dope-smuggling center, but most of the drugs carried into the United States from Fujardo and other ports in Puerto Rico were taken in by boat. When he'd first heard about the job from Player and the man in New York, he'd had a brief suspicion that his passengers might have been drug smugglers, but it really didn't seem likely. There were plenty of better and less expensive ways to smuggle drugs than to hire a venture pilot.

Still, China didn't really like the story about the customers being South American political refugees. It didn't smell right. Cuba was one thing—not so long ago, the only way out of there for some people had been through daring pickups off the beach. But these customers were damn near in the States already.

He quit worrying about it, collected his gear and went on up to the little shack that served as the office for the Fujardo flying service. Inside he checked in with the bored-looking clerk, paid an overnight parking fee on the Apache and called a cab. It was eleven o'clock and he wasn't supposed to meet his customers until noon; he could use the extra hour to have a few beers and relax a little.

Riding in, he remembered the little town from another visit about three years ago. It was an ordinary Caribbean town of about four thousand natives that swelled to twice that size in the winter months when the rich yachtsmen and tourists came flooding in. As they entered the town, he noticed a little white building sitting off by itself down by the waterfront. A sign on the front said it was the Texas Cafe and Saloon. There was a big house trailer sitting behind the cafe and China wondered what expatriate from Texas had come to Puerto Rico to try and sell Lone Star beer and chicken fried steaks.

China got out at the Miramar Restaurant, an ordinary Puerto Rican tourist cafe and drinking bar that the clients had chosen as the rendezvous point. He stopped just inside the door, letting his eyes adjust to the dimness. It was too early for a lunch crowd, but a few tables were occupied. He selected one near the back wall with a good view of the front door and sat down. A waiter came over and he told him just to bring him a beer and a tall glass. Then he lit a cigarette and settled down to wait. Overhead several fans stirred the warm air and a few flies buzzed around the bowls of hot sauce that sat on every table. The waiter brought his beer and went back to join the other waiters leaning against the bar. China drank off the beer, upended the glass and set it in front of him. It was the recognition signal. He did not expect his customers to be early, but he might as well be ready.

He was in the midst of his second beer when he saw a man come through the door and stop and look slowly around. The man was small and dressed in a light blue suit. Even from the distance China could see that he had dark, slicked-back hair and a small mustache. He was wearing dark glasses. After a second he took them off and looked around the room again. China moved the glass across the table. The man put his glasses back on and came over to the table. He said, in good English, but with a Spanish accent, "You are the pilot?"

"Yes," China said. "Sit down."

The man pulled out a chair and sat down opposite China. Before he spoke, he reached inside his coat pocket, took out a pack of cigarettes and lit one. The little movement had exposed a glimpse of a shoulder holster to China. He wondered if the man had done it deliberately. When his cigarette was burning, the man said, "You can call me Cortez."

"All right," China said. "I'll call you Cortez. You can call me China Blue. Because that's my name." He studied the man, thinking he looked more like a Spanish Harlem pimp than a hot-shot political fugitive. But then, China reminded himself, he didn't really know what a Spanish Harlem pimp looked like.

"Your plane is ready?" the man asked. "It is the correct type and size? There will be four of us."

"I understood that," China said. "You just leave the plane to me. I want to know all there is to know about this job. Where are the rest of your people? I didn't know I'd see just one of you."

The man made an impatient gesture. All his movements were nervous and jerky. He said, "We can speak of that later. Right now it is important that we prepare to leave as soon as possible. Let us go to the airfield now. I will make arrangements for my countrymen to meet us there."

China gave a short laugh. He hadn't liked the looks of the man and he was liking what he was saying even less. He said, "Just take it a little slower there, partner. I'm not going anywhere until I know all the details about the job and exactly who it is I'll be flying. And we're not going to do that out at the airport; we're going to do it right here. You want a drink of something?"

The waiter had come over and was standing there expectantly. The man waved his hand impatiently, "No, no," he said.

But China said to the waiter, "Bring us a couple of beers." When the waiter was gone, he said, "Makes you look a little conspicuous if you don't order something when you're sitting at a table in a joint where they sell food and drink."

"All right, all right," the man said. He waved his hand again. "Just as you say. But I would like to make arrangements just as soon as possible to leave. Can we be away in two hours?"

"Today?" China sat back in his chair. "My understanding was that you wanted to leave tomorrow."

"That has all changed. It is dangerous for us here. We'd like to be away as soon as possible."

China regarded him for a long moment, sipping beer. He said, "How long you been here? Here in Puerto Rico."

"Two days."

"Then I don't see where one more day would make any difference."

"Yes," the man insisted. "We would like to leave today."

China made up his mind. He shook his head. "I'm sorry, that's not possible. Even if we get all our business settled. There's a weather front between here and the mainland, a line of thunderstorms that won't break up until very late tonight. We couldn't make it through."

The waiter brought the round of beer and the man sat there rubbing his hand over his slicked-back hair until he was gone. Then he said, "We will go around them."

China shook his head. "It's a solid line. We'd have to fly five hundred miles out of the way to make an end run. It can't be done." He was partially lying, but he didn't like the way the man was trying to rush him.

Cortez said, "Then we will go through them."

China gave a short laugh. "*You* may go through them," he said. "This cowboy isn't. I've tried to fly through one line of solid thunderstorms and that was one too many."

The man looked nervous. He fidgeted in his seat and played with a gold ring on his finger. But, China noted, he didn't glance over his shoulder or look around the room to see who might be there. And a man who'd suddenly developed a fear that an enemy might be at hand would do that. So China could not understand the immediate need to leave. It didn't make sense. Cortez finally said, "Then when could we leave? At the earliest?"

China said, "I assume you still want to fly north? To the mainland?"

"Yes, that is correct. That has not changed."

"Then in the morning. In the Caribbean and other hot

places near water thunderstorms build up in the afternoon because of the heat and the humidity. Then they dissipate at night when the air cools off. We could leave as early in the morning as you wanted to. Right at dawn.''

The man looked unhappy. He got out a cigarette and lit it. Finally he made a nervous pass of his hand through the air. ''I was told that your organization had the best pilots, that you could accomplish the very difficult. It was for that reason that we contacted you. Now you say you cannot do the difficult.''

''The difficult, yes,'' China said dryly, ''the impossible, no. But don't feel bound by any contract to us, señor. You just feel free to make any other arrangements you want to make. As far as I'm concerned, you and I can call the whole deal off right now.''

''No, no, no,'' the man said, holding up a hand. ''Do not be hasty. Besides, where would I get a pilot and plane in Puerto Rico at this late time?''

''That's your problem,'' China said. ''I'm telling you what I'll do. If it don't suit you, you can get another outfit.''

''No,'' the man said. ''You cannot do that. You cannot leave us in such a difficult fix. We have made a contract with your boss in New York. We are paying you a great deal of money for this. We expect the best.''

''I agree about the money,'' China said. ''We're not cheap. But don't complain to me about it. That's not my department.''

''All right, all right,'' the man said. ''Just as you say. You will have your money. We have it with us. In cash.''

''And about that money,'' China said. ''I'll need half of it today. Six thousand in advance.''

''Of course,'' the man said. ''That was the agreement.'' He waved his hand and leaned back in his chair. ''I will give it to you as we board the plane in the morning.''

China shook his head. "No you won't. You'll give it to me today. While the telegraph office is still open. That is, if you want me to do this job, you will."

The man sat forward in his chair. "I do not understand this! Why should I hand over six thousand dollars of the people's money to you, a stranger? I will give it to you as we board."

"No," China said. "No deal. Today, cash, before the telegraph office closes."

Cortez said, "I do not know you. How do I know you won't simply leave with our money? What assurances can you give me?"

"None. Except our reputation. You can take it or leave it." China picked up his beer bottle and took a long drink. "Point is, I know me, but I don't know you. I trust me, but I don't trust you."

Cortez pulled his head back. "That is insulting, señor."

China shrugged. "Be as insulted as you want to be. It's one of our rules. A few years back a gent paid one of our pilots as he was boarding. Then, when our pilot landed him in a very out-of-the-way place, the man produced a pistol and took his money back—and handcuffed our pilot to the strut of the landing gear. He spent a long day and night there before anyone found him. By that time the man was long gone and the pilot was out his money, plus being out a hell of a hard night. So we don't do it that way anymore." He looked directly at Cortez. "Now, I get the money and take it to the telegraph office and wire it off to wherever I'm sending it and that way I don't have it on me when we land wherever we're going." He took another sip of beer. "And that way you ain't tempted to use that pistol you got in that shoulder holster to try and get a free ride. *Comprende*?"

Cortez ignored the remark about the shoulder holster.

He got out a cigarette and lit it. "How do I know you won't take the people's money and leave?"

"You asked that once. I told you there aren't any assurances except our honor. Now, you take it or leave it. I'm very frankly getting tired of talking to you. So either come up with the money right now or quit wasting my time."

The man thought for a moment, running his hand nervously over his slicked-back hair. Finally he said, "Very well. I agree. You will have the money."

"When?"

"Later this afternoon. I will go to the hotel and get it. I will bring it to you here."

"All right. That part's fine. Now tell me where we're going and what this job is all about."

From the inside of his pocket the man took out a folded area map. He spread it out on the table and China saw it was a sectional chart of the Atlanta area. The man smoothed it and pointed to a penciled X near a little town named Ammonsville, about thirty miles outside of Atlanta.

China turned the chart so he could see it better. It was obviously a very small town, but it had a little local airport with a three-thousand-foot sod airstrip. From experience China knew it was the kind of place that would house three or four local planes and have no full-time air service station. There'd be a phone at the shack of the local fixed base operator with instructions on whom to call to come out and give you some gas. He was used to landing people who didn't want to announce their arrival in the U.S. at out-of-the-way places like that.

China picked up the map, folded it, and handed it back to the man. "All right," he said, "I can handle that. Then what? I understand this is a round trip with a layover. How long a layover?"

"Layover? What does that mean?"

"How long am I going to have to wait for you at that airport? How long is your business going to take?"

"Ah, yes. Twenty-four hours. Perhaps forty-eight. No more."

China shook his head. "Too long. I understood twenty-four hours. That's it. I'm going to be enough of a topic of conversation around that place as it is. I want to get in and out of there as fast as possible." He wanted to ask the man their business in Ammonsville—or, more likely, their business in Atlanta—but he didn't say anything. That was part of the service. But he did say, "You understand, I don't carry drugs. And you understand that I don't engage in anything against my own principles."

"Exactly what does that mean, your own principles?"

China said, "That means if you and your partners are going in there to rob a bank or something and you come back with the police after you, I'm going to take off without you. You savvy? I'm not indulging you or any other passenger in that kind of service."

"No, no, no," the man said. "It is all political. We go there to pick up a countryman, a political leader who has been in exile. That is why we will be four. We will be three going, but four returning."

"You keep saying the people's money. You ain't communists are you? I don't like communists."

The little man drew himself up. "We are liberators, señor. Revolutionaries who seek to free an oppressed people."

"I'll just bet," China said dryly. "Probably even if they don't want to be freed by you. But that's none of my business how you people run your goddam country. Where do we return? Here?"

"No," the man said. "We return to Nicaragua."

Chapter Seven

"Nicaragua?" China said. He rubbed his chin. "I don't know about Nicaragua. I hadn't counted on that. That place is in a hell of a mess right now. There's a lot of people shooting off guns over there."

Cortez said, "That was the agreement."

China shook his head. "No, that wasn't the agreement. Nobody mentioned Nicaragua." But he couldn't say it very convincingly. The hell of it was that he'd taken the job so hastily, and time had been so short that he really hadn't gotten the full details. Player had probably known all the job entailed, but he'd been sick and the man in New York had probably assumed Player had relayed all the necessary information. Well, he was doing what he was always warning Player against; he was gambling. He wasn't taking calculated risks, but gambling by operating on very scanty information. He sat there thinking. Finally he said, "Well, I'm not landing you at any airport in Nicaragua.

133

I'll land you on a beach somewhere, but that's the best I'll do.''

The man looked a little surprised. "But that was the agreement. That you would land us on a beach. We ourselves have no desire to land at an airport, no matter how small.''

"Well," China said, "then we have no problem. You run along and get the money and we're in business.''

"Why don't you come with me? It's at the Palomar Hotel. Only a very short walk from here.''

"Fine," China said. "That'll give me a chance to see the other people I'll be flying." He got up and signaled for the waiter. "You go on outside and wait. I'll be right there as soon as I pay.''

When he came out of the restaurant, Cortez was standing on the sidewalk. He looked worried. He said, "By the way, señor, what hotel are you staying at?''

They were walking down the sidewalk. China said, "I don't have a place to stay yet. I'll find one.''

Cortez said, "The Palomar is first class. Perhaps we can find you a room there. The town is very full. It is the tourist season, I believe.''

"No, thanks" China said. "I'll find a place on my own.''

"You will let me know where that will be? In case I have to reach you?''

"Oh, sure," China said, not meaning a word of it. "But don't you worry about reaching me. If you don't hear different before tomorrow morning, you just figure to be out at that airport about dawn.''

"But what if there is an emergency, a change of plan?''

China gave him a look. "There's not going to be any change of plans, not any plans that are going to include me and the airplane." Then he reached over and tapped Cortez on the left breast, where the shoulder holster hung.

"And by the way, you're going to have to turn that little trinket over to me before I board you. That one and any others your people might have. I'll give them back to you once you're out of the airplane. But it makes me nervous to fly people who are carrying guns."

The man gave him a look, but didn't say anything. They were at the Palomar by then. Like the few other hotels in Fujardo, it was just a small two-story building with a tiny lobby. China started through the door with the man, but Cortez stopped him. He said, "No, you wait here. I will deliver the money to you."

China said, "I wanted to see my other passengers."

The man said, "Tomorrow. They are sleeping now."

China said, "All right, but just remember, if I don't like their looks, I might not take you. You said there's one other man and a woman. And that we'll be picking up another man in Georgia. Is that correct?"

"Yes, that is correct," Cortez said. "Three men and one woman. There will be no problems." He hesitated and then said, "The lady became a little sick in the boat coming to this island. But she should be better by tomorrow."

China said, "I don't want anybody throwing up in the airplane. You better get her well by morning."

"She is not that kind of sick," Cortez said. "She will be all right, I assure you."

He went through the door and China waited on the street. Cortez was gone about ten minutes. He came back with an envelope and an unhappy look on his face. China held out his hand for the envelope, but Cortez said, "My countryman is not pleased. He had expected we would be gone today. There is the woman. She is very anxious."

China said, "Why should she be any more anxious than you and the other guy?"

The little Latin American said, "She, uh, has a personal relation with the man we are to pick up."

"She his wife?"

"Uh, very close to it."

China shrugged. "Well, I don't care if she's his grandmother. We still aren't going until the morning."

Reluctantly Cortez handed over the envelope. China took a quick look inside. He didn't count it, but he could tell it was several thousands of dollars, in cash.

Cortez said, "It is all there, señor."

"I'm sure it is," China said. He put the envelope in his shirt pocket. "The telegraph operator will count it when he sends off the money order."

Then he told Cortez where to meet him the next morning. He said, "It's a Piper Aztec, red and white, parked in the row of airplanes nearest to the landing strip. You can't miss it because it's the only red and white one there. The plane's number is N 5510. That number is in big letters on the fuselage. I'll meet you at six a.m. sharp. Don't have the cab driver take you right to the airplane. Get out at the little airport office shack. It's only about a fifty-yard walk from there."

Cortez said, sounding anxious, "And you will very certainly be there?"

"*Certemente*," China said. For a moment he gave Cortex a long, appraising look. "Amigo," he said, "you know, this is none of my business, but you don't strike me as one of those fire-breathing revolutionaries. You look more like the chief accountant for a tamale company. You sure you know what you're into?"

Cortez gave him a flat look, a look that caused China to suddenly think he might have misread his man. "Oh yes," the Latin American said, "I know what I am doing. We all do. But for your surprise, even though it is none of your business, as you say, I studied accounting at City College in New York. I almost became an American citizen."

China reached out and touched the man's left breast. "And you know how to use that piece of machinery you are carrying?"

"Very well," the man said. He smiled thinly. "And we will expect you to be there and to perform the job we are paying you for."

"Don't worry about that," China said. He was studying the man closer, almost certain now that he didn't know his customer as well as he'd thought. He said, "What about the other guy? The one in the hotel. You're an accountant; what the hell is he, an economics professor or a lawyer?"

"He is a specialist," Cortez said.

"A specialist in what?"

"Just a specialist. You have your specialty, which is flying, and he has his."

"And the woman's specialty is *amor*? Is that right?"

The man smiled thinly again and turned back to the door of the hotel. But just before he went in, he said, "You know, señor China Blue, we are not worried about you leaving with our money. Your plane is being watched even right now. We saw you land. And I verified you were the one we were expecting when I went upstairs to get the money. I telephoned."

China said, "Boy, I'm impressed. You guys are a bunch of hot-shot organizers. Country boy like me is just pleased as punch to get to hang around with you."

Again that thin smile, and then Cortez disappeared into the hotel. China watched him mount the stairs to the second floor and then turned away.

He found a cab, went to the telegraph office, and wired the money off to the man in New York. Having done that, he had an afternoon and evening to kill with no special plans. He'd left his bags at the little airport office and he

figured he might as well retrieve them. After that he'd find
a hotel room and get something to eat. All he'd had so far
was the breakfast he'd shared with Cliff Finch.

At the airport, he didn't check to see if his plane was
being watched. It didn't make any difference to him whether
it was or not. He was curious, however, as to whether
Cortez had been telling the truth about spotting him as he
landed. He doubted that. They didn't seem all that well-
organized. Probably their whole revolutionary movement
consisted of nine guys and a second-hand mimeographing
machine.

Still they did have a loose twelve thousand dollars.
Riding back in, he asked the driver to take him to an
out-of-the-way hotel. The driver shrugged. "There are
only four, señor. Fujardo is very small."

The driver took him to the La Casa hotel. He got a room
on the second floor with no difficulty, then took his bags
up and let himself in. It was a typical room, a short
entrance hall with the bathroom on the immediate left,
then a small room with a single bed and a small table.
There was no TV. A French door opened onto a balcony.
The room was not air-conditioned and the doors were
standing open. China put his bags down and crossed the
room and stepped out onto the balcony. The hotel was
built on a courtyard. Down below he could see a dirt floor
with several fountains placed about and here and there a
concrete bench. There were a few trees growing in the
corners, none of which he knew the names of. It looked
like a hundred other little hotels he'd stayed in south of the
border. He did notice that the wrought-iron railing around
his little balcony was loose, the old concrete beginning to
crumble and let go the bolts that held it in place.

He went back in the room and decided he was hungrier
than he was dirty. But before he went out to eat, he took a
careful survey of the room to see where he could hide

certain things, such as his .357 revolver and the emergency cash. There were no good places in the bathroom. The toilet had a European-type water chest high on the wall, but anyone who knew anything about searching a room would look there first. In the bedroom there was nothing but the little table, a rickety chair and a scarred bureau with a little mirror behind it. The bed was a box-springs-and-mattress affair and it looked as if the bed would have to do. He got down on the floor and wiggled under the bed. Then, with his pocket knife, he cut a little hole in the bottom of the box springs and worked his gun and the extra cash inside. He was satisfied with the hiding place. Someone would look under the mattress and might even possibly inspect the box springs, but he'd made his cut just inside the corner where the wooden support joined the outside frame and they'd have a hard time finding that. Besides, he didn't expect his room to be searched. It was just an old habit he'd developed from the time he'd been left high and dry in a hotel in Vancouver with no passport and no cash and no credit cards. He hadn't expected his room to be broken into then, either.

After that he went out of the hotel and stood on the sidewalk looking around. There, right across the street, and cater-corner, was the little frame resturant he'd noticed coming in from the airport: the Texas Cafe and Saloon. It seemed as good a place as any to get something to eat, though he doubted that the cafe or its management knew the first thing about Texas.

He crossed the street and went in, stopping just inside the door to look the place over. It was just a small, square room with a half-dozen tables. But it was well-lit from the big windows on three sides. To the back was a bar with a few stools and a service window behind it, obviously leading off the kitchen. The place was empty except for a man standing behind the bar.

As China stood there, the man said, "C'mon in, cowboy. Where's your hat?"

China waited until he'd got to the bar and sat down on one of the stools before he answered. He said, "Well, to tell you the truth, I wear nothing but three-hundred-and-fifty-dollar hats, but I never wear them outside of Texas because nobody but a Texan can appreciate them. And what's the point of wearing a three-hundred-fifty-dollar hat if some yokel in Puerto Rico is going to think it cost ten dollars?"

"Damn good thinking," the man said. He was tall and spare with a red face and a ring of white hair around his balding head. China judged him to be in his mid-fifties, but he could see from the square chest and the biceps that still bulged slightly from the sleeves of the white T-shirt he was wearing that the man had once been a pretty stout hombre. The man said, "What part of Texas you from?"

China named his home and then said, "You know it?"

"Hell, no," the man said. "I couldn't find Texas on a road map. Never been in the state in my life."

"You own this place?"

The man said, "You see anybody else around here dumb enough to claim it?"

"Well, if you own it and you've never seen Texas, how come the name?"

The man wiped his hands on the white butcher's apron he was wearing. "Previous owner claimed the name drew customers." He snorted. "This goddam place wouldn't draw flies if you named it Drinks on the House. What'll you have?"

"Beer," China said. He motioned at a wooden sign hanging behind the bar. Burned into the wood was the legend: FREE BEER TOMORROW. "That sign true?"

"Every day," the man said. "You come back tomorrow and it will still say the same thing. Story of my life.

Tomorrow never comes." He rummaged in an ice chest and came out with a bottle of Texas beer. "Hope you can drink this horse piss," he said as he uncapped the bottle and set it in front of China. "I can't give it away. You want a glass?"

"Yeah," China said. "I been roughing it all day. Think I'll take it easy for a while."

"Shit," the man said. "Sloth and indolence are the watchwords around this place." He took a cold pilsner glass out of the crushed ice and set it in front of China. "There, over-indulge yourself. Be seduced by the good life."

China smiled slightly. "You also serve food here? I'd like to eat a little lunch."

"God almighty," the man said, "you must be a stranger." He took a towel and mopped the bar in front of China. "You must have just come into town without being warned. Yes, we serve food here, such as it is. The special today is beef stew, but that'll make you just about as sick as everything else on the menu. You can have steak or a hamburger or nearly anything you want. Doesn't matter what you order, it all tastes the same."

"The beef stew sounds all right. I'll try some of that."

The man turned and yelled through the service window. "Olga! Another victim! The special, God rest his soul."

He turned back to China and put out his hand. "My name's Jungle Jim, Jungle Jim Wilcox."

China shook the large hand. "That's a strange name. Were you in the movies? Tarzan, maybe?"

"No," the man said, "Elmo Lincoln beat me out on that. He was the first, back in 1930. No, what happened was, during World War II, I happened to find myself on Iwo Jima and I managed to get lost about fifty yards from my platoon bivouac. I believe they gave me that name in honor of the fact that I was not real versed in jungle skills. I've carried it around ever since as a penance."

China drank beer and then lit a cigarette. He said, "I can understand the feeling. I have been lost occasionally myself."

"You lost now?" Jim was looking at him, his head cocked to one side. "You don't look like a tourist. And you look like too smart a man to come to a place like this to make any money."

China said, "I fly people. People who don't want to take the airlines."

"Ah," Jim said, "A pilot. A man of skill. Wish to hell I had one. A skill, that is."

Just then a loud bell sounded in the service window. Jim jumped and swore. "Goddam that woman!" he said. "She does that just for meanness. She could say softly, 'Sweetheart, the order is ready.' But she'd rather give me a near heart attack with that goddam bell. One of these days . . .''

He got the plate and set it in front of China, adding a napkin and a knife and fork. He said, "You might as well eat up here at the bar. I need someone to talk to."

China had caught a glimpse through the serving window of a woman's wide, pleasant face surrounded by blonde curls. He said, "The cook don't look like she has a bad heart."

Jim said, "Hah, you ought to live with her. That's my old lady." He turned and yelled through the window. "Olga, come out here and expose yourself. To public ridicule, that is."

The stew was delicious, as China had expected it would be. It came on a plate with a fresh salad and small, crispy rolls on the side. There was real butter to go with the rolls. China suspected that a large lunch crowd had left not too long before. He said, as he ate, "Jungle Jim, I think you are a bullshitter."

"Yes, he is a bullshitter."

China turned his head. A woman in a white cook's dress was coming through the kitchen door. She took a kerchief off her head and shook out her blonde hair. It was the pleasant-faced woman China had seen through the service window. She came around the bar and he could see that she was a little plump, but still a very attractive woman. She looked to be in her mid-thirties. She climbed up on the stool next to China. "Yes," she said, "he is the worst bullshitter in the world."

China said: "Well, a man ought to try and be the best at whatever he does."

She said, "He is the best at what he does. Believe me." She had a slight German accent.

Jungle Jim said, "Meet China Blue. Pilot China Blue. Of Texas."

"How do you do," she said. She put out a plump, soft hand. "My name is Olga Knoopf."

China noted they had different last names. He assumed the woman wasn't Jungle Jim's wife, that she just lived with him.

It turned into a very pleasant afternoon. The food and the friendly company were making China feel better. He'd been worried and bothered about the job facing him, partly because of tiredness, but mostly because he didn't like the feel of it. The rest in the little cafe was helping him.

After a while he and Jungle Jim went to sit at a table in front of a window overlooking the harbor. Olga took over as bartender for the few customers that came wandering in. They sat there looking out at the sea and the boats. Jim said, "I run a little tour service also. Take the tourists that can't afford the charter boats out to see the sunset on the water. Strictly for the poor man. Got a little motor-driven trimaran and I run them around the bay for the supper cruise of sandwiches and beer, let them see the sunset on the great blue water and then bring them back in. It's a living.''

"You like it?"

"It beats Cinncinnati and points east and west. Actually, it ain't so bad. Olga really runs the cafe. I just spread the goodwill and the bullshit." He looked at his watch. "Tour's going out in about an hour. At six thirty. Want to come along? On the house, professional courtesy from one tour guide to another."

China shook his head. "No thanks, Jim. I got a few things to do and a few phone calls to make and then I'm going to turn in early. I didn't get much sleep last night and I got an early morning flight."

"Taking off tomorrow, huh? You get back this way much?"

"Yeah, I do quite a bit of charter work in the Caribbean. I guess the same people who can afford these islands are the ones who can afford us."

Jim said, "Well, if you're ever in town late, and need a last beer, me and the old lady live in that house trailer right behind the cafe. This town shuts down early, but we go on to all hours. Just knock on the door."

"Thanks," he said. "Might take you up on that some time."

He left not too long afterwards. Walking back to his hotel, he tried to think of a good reason to tell Bonnie why he hadn't called her sooner. She was going to be angry as hell, and no mistake. He knew he should have done it before, knew she would be worried, but it seemed with one thing and another he hadn't quite found the right moment.

It took a few moments to get the call through, but then she came on, sounding a little breathless, as if she'd come running in from outside. He said, making his voice cheerful, "Hi, babe, how's it going?"

There was a pause and then she said, "Blue, you rotten son-of-a-bitch, you better have a goddam good reason why you haven't called me before now!"

"Well, hell," he said, "I been on the move. Shit, Bonnie, you know this life. I—"

"Don't bullshit me, Blue! I wouldn't even know if you were alive or dead or where you were or anything if Jane hadn't happened to call me and I found out from her that Player was in the hospital and you'd taken his assignment. *She* was shocked! She had expected me to already know what was going on! She just called to talk. How in the hell do you think that made *me* feel! You are the most no-good bastard I have ever—"

"Now wait," he said. "Now wait just a minute, Bonnie. Just stop yelling and listen for a moment."

There was a sudden silence on the line. She said quietly, "All right."

"Now, look, I'm sorry I worried you. But I haven't had a chance to call. Not up until now."

She said, "Have you been in jail?"

"No, of course not."

"Have you been unconscious?"

"All right," he said. "Now c'mon."

"You been paralyzed? Kidnapped? Marooned somewhere?"

"Ha ha," he said. "Very funny. Just go on with your goddam silly remarks."

"Blue, why the fuck didn't you call me! Player got you out of Mexico thirty-six fucking hours ago! What, you couldn't find five minutes to pick up a phone and call me?"

"You sound like a Jewish mother," he said. "Listen, the reason I didn't call you before was I wanted to wait until I got here to Puerto Rico to see what the job would be like and to know how long I'd be gone. I knew you'd have about nine thousand questions and I wanted to be able to answer—''

"What does the job look like?"

"See what I mean?"

"All right, all right. You made your point. Now, what about the assignment? Jane said Player didn't tell her anything about it. Does it look rough?"

He thought for a moment and then he said, "Yeah, pretty shaky. I'm not liking the look of it at all."

There was silence on the other end of the phone for a long second and then she said, "Whaaat? What are you saying?"

"I said I don't like the look of it too much. There's three men and a woman and the job may take three or four days. They claim to be South American refugees, but they all got guns and they want to go to Georgia and then return. I get the feeling they're going down there to rob a bank and then get back to the airport for their getaway with me sitting there with the engines ticking over."

He could hear her take a little breath. She said, "Blue, are you serious?"

"Of course, I'm serious. Why shouldn't I be serious?"

"Well, uh, uh, because you always tell me every run's a piece of cake, a milk run. What happened to those? Even when you know it's going to be rough, you always tell me a lie."

"Hell, I thought you wanted the truth. You wanted the truth about why I didn't call you and then you didn't believe me when I told you the truth about that."

She laughed, a sound of relief in her voice. "Oh, I get it now. This is to make me believe your other story. All of a sudden you're Mister No Lie, Mister Truth Teller. What you really got is a milk run, so you're telling me it's going to be dangerous so that I won't be mad anymore and will be waiting anxiously. That's it, isn't it?"

He made his voice sound puzzled. "Bonnie, I don't know what you mean. You asked me a question and I told you. Oh, I see now. Okay, you tell me what you want to hear and I'll tell you that. Is that how we do it?"

She was quiet for a few seconds and then she said, her voice uncertain, "Damn you, Blue, you're doing it to me again. Now I don't know what to believe. Now what's the job really like?"

"A milk run," he said. "Piece of cake. Now shut up. How's Player? Did Jane know?"

"He's doing fine. He'll be home in a couple of days. How about you, when you coming home?"

"Pretty soon. How are things around the old homestead? Stock doing all right?"

"Yes, now tell me exactly when you're coming home?"

He said, "Must be pretty soon. I miss you."

Her surprise vibrated along the phone wire.

"You miss me? Blue, are you drunk? You never tell me that. You must be drunk."

"No, I just miss you. Look, I got to get off this phone and get some sleep. I got an early flight. I'll be home in two or three days."

"Call me when you can." Her voice got soft. "I love you."

"I love you, too."

He was asleep almost as soon as he lay his head on the pillow. He hadn't bothered to leave a wake-up call, for he knew his own mental alarm clock was a lot more dependable than the desk service in the little hotel.

He went to sleep hoping that Bonnie wouldn't worry too much and that he could get the damn assignment over with in a hurry and get back home and have some time to relax.

Chapter Eight

He awoke in the darkness, straining to read the luminous dial of his watch. For a moment he squinted at it, still too sleepy to make out the numbers. It was five o'clock.

He sat up on the side of the bed and yawned. Still drowsy, he pushed off the bed and stumbled into the bathroom and turned on the shower. He let it get just warm enough to be endurable and then stepped into the stinging spray and stood for a time. When he was good and awake he stepped out, dried off and then shaved. Ten minutes later he was dressed and down at the motel desk trying to pay off a half-asleep night clerk who couldn't get his bill sorted out. After that it took more time to get a taxi called. Finally he was on his way out to the airport.

The sun was just coming up when he got out of the cab. The grass around the plane was slack with dew as he carried his bags over to the side of the airplane and set them down by the baggage compartment. He yawned and

lit a cigarette. He felt good. It was time to be flying back
to the States. The only thing missing was that he was not
flying back to Texas.

He smoked a moment and then flicked the cigarette
away and did a walk-around check of the airplane. Everything looked fine. He climbed into the cockpit and did a
visual check of the instruments. Then he got out and
opened the cowling on each engine and looked inside.
After a visual check he pulled out the dipsticks in each
engine and checked the oil. It was up to the proper level.
After that he closed and locked the cowling. The airplane
was ready to fly.

He lounged against the side of the fuselage, waiting for
his passengers. The light had come stealing across the field
as the sun had risen, and now he could see beyond the
rows of airplanes to the little flight service station shack.
As he watched, he saw the lights of a car come slowly up
to the operations shack and stop. He heard doors being
slammed and faint voices in the morning air. He wished
mightily that he could have had something cold to drink,
but the Coke machine in the lobby of the hotel had been
out of order, so he'd just taken a drink of water and gone
on.

Watching, he could see several people threading their
way through the line of aircraft. He assumed they were his
passengers, but he couldn't quite make them out. As they
got nearer though, he could see that it was in fact two men
with a woman in the middle.

He stepped back and got his instrument case and shoved
it into the airplane. Then he opened the luggage compartment.
He picked his two bags up, his flight kit and clothes bag,
and waited as the trio came toward him.

"Cortez?" China said.

"Yes. We are here."

They came around the wing of the nearest airplane.

China set his bags down. The two men were supporting the woman between them. She seemed barely able to walk. Her head was half thrown back on her shoulders and her legs were rubbery. It was good light now and China could see all three of them clearly. Cortez was to her left; the man to her right was bigger than Cortez, but dressed much the same, even to the light blue suit and the carefully knotted tie. They stopped right in front of China. Cortez said, "We just have these two bags. Let us depart. We are ready to go."

China was looking at the woman. The two men had her by the arms and were holding her shoulders straight. But her head was lolling back and forth. He could see, even as slack as her body was, that she was young and beautiful. She looked Spanish because she was dark, but she could have been any nationality. He said, "Well now, just wait a goddam minute. This lady is sick. What's the matter with her?"

Cortez said, "It is nothing. I told you she was a bit under the weather. Let us get aboard."

China said, "Just hold up a minute. What the hell's going on here? What's the matter with her?"

The other man, the man on the woman's right, said, "You have been hired, pilot. You fly the airplane. Do not ask questions."

His voice was deeper than Cortez's and more authoritative. Now that they were closer, China could see that he was wearing a double-breasted suit. The thought ran through his mind: A double-breasted suit hides a shoulder holster much better. He said, "That woman is either drunk or she's been drugged. And it's too damn early in the morning for her to be drunk."

Cortez said, "This is none of your concern. You have been hired to fly the airplane. You will fly us as agreed."

"The hell I will," China said. He was looking hard at

the woman, noting the graceful lines of her face as she swayed back and forth against the two men. Her black hair looked shoulder length, but it was difficult to tell the way her head bobbed back and forth. She was wearing a simply cut gray dress. Even in the dawn's light China could tell it was silk. He said, "I'm not carrying that woman. And I'm not carrying either one of you."

The bigger man said, "We have paid you, China Blue. Put our luggage in the plane and we will put this woman in the back. She's not your business."

China said flatly, "Anybody I carry in an airplane is my business. And I'm telling you I will not carry this woman in this shape. Hell, she can't even talk."

Cortez said excitedly, "I told you she was sick. We must get her to a doctor in the United States."

China said, "Bullshit. She ain't sick; she's doped to the eyes. If she was that sick, you'd have her to a doctor here in Puerto Rico. They got them here."

Cortez said, "Your attention, señor. We have paid you six thousand dollars in advance. Now live up to your agreement."

China reached down and picked up his bags. "You can get your six thousand back tomorrow. Or however long it takes me to get it here. Or you can bring that woman back tomorrow, or even later today when she's able to talk and tell me she wants to go. But right now I ain't carrying her. So far as I know, she's being kidnapped."

Cortez said, "Señor, you must take us! We are ready to go. We have an agreement with your boss."

"I done told you," China said, "he ain't my boss. I'm the one decides who goes in any airplane I'm flying."

The bigger man said, "Enough of this." In a fluid move he suddenly reached inside his jacket and came out with an automatic pistol. He pointed it at China. "You will fly us. No more of this talk."

China stared at the gun that was pointing at him. He thought: Damn, that's a Baretta 9mm. That gun is strictly gun-runner black market. These boys are probably heavy-weight terrorists. That gun comes straight from Cuba.

He said, "Shit, whatever you say." And then, without a pause, he swung his left hand around, catching the gun-man in the chest with the thrown suitcase. He heard an oath, but the gun did not fire, and he was off, running through the lines of airplanes, ducking and dodging, expecting a shot to follow him at any second.

But none came. He drew up in front of the little flight service shack, breathing hard from the run he'd made. He ducked inside the door. The day man was just coming on duty. He yawned and said, "May I help you?"

China was looking out the window to the flight line. He said, "Call me a taxi cab. Right now. Tell them to hurry."

Then he stepped outside the tiny office and set his flight kit down and rummaged inside for his .357 revolver. With it in hand he scanned the lines of planes, looking for the two men. They were nowhere in sight, which suited him just fine. He hoped they didn't show up, because if they did he was going to have to shoot. And he didn't want any trouble. All he wanted to do was forget the whole goddam deal and go home to Texas.

The cab came soon enough and he got in and directed the driver toward town. He'd shoved the revolver down in his belt, but he had the driver stop and wait as he looked out the back window for any pursuit. There were no other cars on the little road that wound by the coast from the airport. After a time he told the driver to go on.

He went back to the hotel he'd stayed in the night before because he didn't really have any place else to go. The desk clerk was surprised, but he gave China a key. China placed a call to the man in New York from the phone in his room. It took an agonizingly long time for the call to get through and then the valet came on the line. China said, "Wake him up. It's important. This is China."

"Yes, sir."

In a moment the man was on the line, snorting and coughing a little. China said, "This run in Puerto Rico. It's bad news. These guys are black hats. They pull guns."

"All right. Where are you?"

"In Fujardo. That's F-U-J-"

The man said, "I know where it is. I know how to spell it. What do you need?"

"Some allies. We got anybody local?"

"I will get on it right away. Are you in any immediate danger?"

"Negative. But if these *banditos* pull another gun on me, mine may go off."

"Do you need an airlift?"

"Shit, no! I can get out of here. I got a plane here. I just want to make goddam certain that if I shoot one, I don't get detained."

"I'll have to go through San Juan," the impersonal voice said. "It could take a little time. But protect yourself. That's understood."

China hung up the phone, not feeling any better. Even with help from New York, if he got into a scuffle, there would be all sorts of inquiries by the local police and a hell of lot of questions to answer. None of that was good for business.

He turned away from the telephone and lit a cigarette, thinking. The best thing was just to sit tight until the bad boys got clear and then go to the airfield and fly the hell back to Texas. True, he had taken their money for a job, their six thousand dollars. He was willing to give it back, but not with guns being pointed at him. Besides, he figured the going penalty for pulling a gun on a venture pilot was three thousand dollars and waving it was at least three thousand dollars more.

So he didn't figure he owed them a goddam thing. Except a quick exit. If they felt they'd been wronged, they always had the phone number of the man in New York and they could take up their case with him.

But sitting there smoking, he thought of the young woman they'd had with them. She'd looked to be in awful bad shape, looked to be on her way to an airplane ride she didn't want to take. But there was nothing he could do about that. It was none of his business. He was a pilot— not a rescuer of females in distress. He'd already done his good deed for the decade by getting that Claudie out of Mexico.

He let time pass until he decided he was hungry. It was almost nine o'clock. He debated about taking his pistol with him to breakfast, but in the end decided it might be more dangerous to have the gun. He was strictly going to be in public places and he didn't think Cortez and company would try anything too obvious.

On the sidewalk he looked carefully all around before crossing the street and cutting up the block to the Texan Cafe. He didn't see anyone, which didn't surprise him over much. But the hell of it was that Fujardo was such a small town it would be difficult to avoid being seen unless he just stayed in his hotel room.

But it didn't really matter. As soon as he'd had breakfast, he was going to take a cab out to the airport and get the hell out of Puerto Rico.

He was disappointed to see that Olga and Jungle Jim weren't in the cafe, but he assumed they worked late and left it to someone else to handle the breakfast crowd. He got a table by the window and ordered chili and eggs when the waitress came to take his order. Then he sat there sipping a Coke and looking out the window at the little harbor and thinking about his luck. From all appearances his luck was not running too hot. He'd lost an airplane, a fee and a consignment in Mexico. And here he'd done just as bad. Boy, he thought, you better pull your horns in. You been leaving your hat wrongside down and the luck has run out of it.

But he could look at it another way. On two seperate occasions he'd had people interested in stopping his clock and though he'd lost fees and airplanes and such, he hadn't lost his life. Maybe his luck was hot as a pistol. It all depended on how you looked at it.

When he was finished with breakfast he went back to his room and collected his gear, then went downstairs and checked out again. The desk clerk was even more confused, but China didn't bother to explain, just asked him to phone for a cab.

China decided to sneak up on the Aztec. He doubted if Cortez or his partner would still be around, but he didn't want to take any chances. After he'd paid off the cab, he stealthily began making his way through the lines of planes toward where his plane was parked. He stopped once to take out the .357 and shove it down in his waistband.

As he cleared the last line of parked aircraft, he could see that no one was around. But he hadn't expected them to be in plain sight. He waited, keeping his eyes moving, trying to spot any sign of movement among the maze of fuselages and wings and vertical stabilizers. Nothing happened. Finally he walked across the open space between rows and went up to the Aztec. Silence. No shouts, no sudden sound of running feet, no gunshots.

"Hell," he said, "looks like the boys have decided to give up and go elsewhere."

But still he was surprised they'd given up so easily. He had their money and he was leaving them high and dry in

Puerto Rico. Maybe they'd just decided it wouldn't be good politics to cause a disturbance.

He started to do a walk-around inspection of the airplane and then stopped almost immediately. The cowling flap over the starboard engine was not buttoned down. He said, "Oh, shit!" and walked over to the engine and raised the flap. One quick look told him that the boys hadn't really given up. The P cable, the ground wire that ran to the magneto, had been jerked loose. His airplane had been very effectively disabled.

He thought: And they probably didn't even know what they were doing. They probably just opened the cowling and grabbed the first wire they saw.

Well, their luck had been good. He and the airplane weren't going anywhere until he got the P cable replaced.

He picked up his bags and trudged up to the hangar by the operations shack. One mechanic was on duty, doing an annual inspection on a Cessna 172. China told him his problem. The mechanic shook his head, taking a moment to wipe his hands on a greasy rag. He said, "Sorry, buddy, I ain't got no P cable for that airplane. I can get one, but it'll have to come out of San Juan."

"How soon?"

The man shrugged. "Well, if I call right now and if we get real lucky, we might get it tomorrow. Or it might be the next day. They's a Piper dealer in San Juan and he ought to have one. It ain't a part hard to get; we just can't stock much here."

"Yeah," China said. Their voices were echoing in the cavernous hangar. He said, "Well, let's call. I got to get out of here as quick as possible."

Walking over to the operations shack to use the phone, the mechanic wondered what could have happened to a P cable. "It ain't exactly something that wears out that quick. It short out? If it did, we might ought to look at your whole magneto system.''

"No," China said, "No need for that. It's just the cable. Someday I'll tell you what happened. Right now it's too embarrassing.''

He rode back to town wondering what the desk clerk was going to say this time. He thought out loud, "Man probably thinks I'm caught in a revolving doorway.''

The driver glanced in his rear view mirror. "What is it, señor? You wish to go someplace else?''

"No," China said, "I'm just losing my mind. Don't worry about it.''

At the hotel he got another key from the dumbfounded desk clerk and went back up to his old room. Inside, he looked around. He said, "I wonder if I have been sentenced to spend the rest of my life in this room!''

He was starting to get a little angry. His life was being fooled with and he didn't like that even when it was being done by people he cottoned to—much less a couple of South American tacos he didn't find all that appealing. He sat down on the side of his bed and lit a cigarette and tried to figure what to do. He could hire a car and go to San Juan and rent an airplane there. Obviously there were none for hire at the field in Fujardo. But that would mean leaving Cliff's plane and he didn't want to do that. He didn't want to do it because of the trouble it would cause Cliff, but mainly he didn't want to do it because he didn't like the feeling of being run out of town by the two gunmen. Needless to say, he couldn't go to the police. The last thing he needed was to get stuck answering a lot of questions.

No, the only logical thing he could do was sit tight until his plane was fixed and then get out. And probably the best way to sit tight was just to stay out of sight as much as possible. Maybe if they didn't see him, they'd figure he'd taken a powder.

At any rate, he had some time to kill. He got the .357 out of his flight kit, pulled up his trouser leg and put the gun inside his boot. Then he put his pants leg back over his boot and stood up. The gun felt awkward. It was too big for a boot gun, but it was the only place he had to hide it on his person. Maybe his nerves were telling on him a little, but he damn sure wasn't going out again without a gun.

He went downstairs and got a cab and told the driver to take him as far up the beach as he could go. His plan was to stay away from the town itself. Let them look for him in vain.

The cab driver said, "Very nice restaurant ten miles up the beach, boss. How you like that?"

"That's great," China said. "Let's go."

The fine restaurant turned out to be part of a cheap resort-type hotel. They had an outdoor bar under a thatched roof and China spent the day out there, drinking beer and staring at the waves as they rolled in. The place was full of vacationing secretaries and school teachers who had bought a package tour of the Caribbean and who were determined that they were having a good time. By the time the sun set, China figured he'd been propositioned at least six times, all in very heavy-handed, amateurish fashion. Bonnie, he'd thought as he'd looked the brood over, fear not.

But, it had been a diversion, even if he had found out more about corporate structures and school systems and Peoria and Kansas City and Topeka than he'd ever wanted to know.

He went back into Fujardo at about ten o'clock. The Texas Cafe was closed and he thought momentarily about going over to Jungle Jim's trailer and taking him up on his offer of a late beer. But he was tired and decided to go on to bed. He stopped at the desk to get a couple of newspapers, then went on up to his room. He undressed, putting his gun and his wallet in his boots. Then he wadded up newspaper pages and spread them over the little entrance hall so that nobody could come through the door during the night without making one hell of a racket and waking him up. Lastly, he opened the double doors to the balcony. It was hot in the room, even that late at night, so he took a cold shower and then crawled into bed wet, letting the evaporating water cool his body. Somewhere off in the night someone was having a party. The sounds of a guitar and yelling and laughter came softly through the opened balcony doors.

But he was too tired and sleepy to let it bother him. He thought of Bonnie, and then he drifted off to sleep.

He did not know how long he'd been asleep when the sound of the paper being crackled underfoot awoke him. He came fully awake in the first instant of sound. Without pause he jumped out of the bed and raced low across the room and through the open balcony doors. As he grabbed the iron railing surrounding the balcony he heard a yell behind him. Without hesitation he vaulted over the railing, holding on to the iron bar as he leaped out into the inky black. The courtyard was twenty feet down. He held to the top railing, trying to figure a way to break his fall, hoping whoever was in his room could not see him. Then he heard footsteps coming across the tile floor and he let go and dropped. As he did, he heard a yell and then the BOOM! BOOM! of a gun. He could see, even as he fell away, the orange muzzle flashes.

He hit hard. There'd been no chance to anticipate his landing because he couldn't see the ground, and he'd been late, hitting almost flat-footed. He'd rolled immediately, but he'd already felt something give in his right foot. But he kept rolling anyway, and as quick as he could he came to his feet and went stumbling, limping, running low for the exit out of the courtyard. He heard the gun fire again and heard a bullet hit something hard and go zinging away. But in the next moment he was through the arched exit from the courtyard and out on the street.

But once there he stopped and looked wildly around, wondering which way to go. He was stark naked, without billfold, without identification, without his gun, without anything. As soon as he'd heard the noise of the paper, his only instinct had been to get out of the room as fast as he could.

But he knew he couldn't stay on the street long. The gunman, or gunmen, would already be going down the stairs. At any moment they could come bursting out of the front of the hotel and he'd be a sitting duck there on the street.

He saw the dim outline of Jungle Jim's cafe, and behind it, his house trailer. Well, they'd invited him in for a late drink. And it was about as late as it could get. He went running across the street, limping on the hard concrete. It felt as if he'd broken the arch in his right foot. He hoped that all he'd done was sprain or bruise it. But for the time being he couldn't worry about that.

It was easier going once he hit the grass behind the cafe. He went straight up to the front door and slumped down, hiding himself as best he could in case the gunmen were already outside looking for him, and knocked desperately at the door. The trailer was dark. Jim said they stayed up late, but looking at his watch, he could see it was nearly three. Maybe they hadn't just gone to bed—maybe they weren't even in. He knocked again, louder, fearfully.

After a moment a dim glow shone in one of the little windows, as if someone had lit a bedside lamp. He knocked again, hearing sounds inside. After a moment a muffled voice came from the other side of the door. "Who is it?"

It sounded like Olga. He said, "It's China Blue. The pilot you met the other day."

She said, "It's very late. I'm in bed."

He said, "Please. I'm in trouble. Please let me in in a hurry." He could see the entrance to the hotel and he was watching it anxiously.

"You said it was the pilot? Mister Blue?"

"Yes," he said urgently. "For God's sake, help me."

He heard a lock being unfastened. He said quickly, "Ma'am, don't be alarmed. I ain't got a stitch on. I'm naked. Let Jim come to the door."

But the door had already swung open. Olga was standing there in a robe. He was huddled at the steps to the door, desperately trying to hide his nakedness, his knees drawn up to his chest. He said, "Olga, please call Jim. I'm naked as a jay bird. I had to jump out of my hotel room window. Some bad hombres are trying to kill me."

She said, "Then get in here." She moved her hand and shut off the light inside the trailer. "Quickly," she said. "I don't care if you are naked."

He got up and scrambled inside the trailer house. She immediately shut the door. He lay on the floor panting slightly. "Wow," he said. "I got some bad business going on. I don't want to involve you folks in it, but could you give me a minute to hide here? And could I maybe borrow a pair of Jim's pants and a shirt?"

She turned on the light. He scrambled to roll up in a ball. "Wait!" he said. "Hell, Olga, I told you I wasn't wearing no clothes. Where the hell is Jim?"

She walked by him, going to a back room. She said, "He is not here. He is gone to San Juan."

He said, "Oh shit! I wouldn't have come busting in here if I'd known Jim wasn't here. Goddam, I'll get out just as quick as I can."

She came back in from the other room and threw him a

sheet. "Here," she said, "cover your body if you are so fastidious. But believe me, I have seen men undressed before."

He gathered the sheet up and wrapped it around himself. He said, "Well, hell, I don't know what to say. I'm kind of embarrassed."

She had gone to sit on a couch against the front wall right by the door. "There is no need," she said. "Now come, tell me of your trouble."

He stood up, holding the sheet around him. "I wonder," he said, "if you'd mind if I took a look out the window first." There was a little high window above the back of the couch. "I'd kind of like to see if anybody saw me come in here."

"Of course," she said. She turned sideways and drew back the little gauzy curtains that hid the glass. He knelt on the couch and peered out. He could just see the front of the hotel and part of the street. Not a soul was in sight. He watched steadily for a few long minutes.

After a time he said, "Damn, I wish I had a cigarette. Didn't have a pocket to bring any along."

"I will get you one," she said. "And would you like a beer?"

"You got any brandy?"

"Yes, of course."

"I'll take about a water glass full of that."

He continued to watch and then he had a lit cigarette shoved in front of his face. Under the sheet she found his hand and drew it out and put the glass of brandy in it. Without taking his eyes away from the window, he took a deep drag of the cigarette and exhaled slowly. "Aaaah," he said. Then he took a drink of the brandy, letting it go down slowly, burning and relaxing his stomach. "Shit," he said, "that tastes good."

She sat back down on the couch. "Who is chasing you? You must tell me about it."

"I'd rather not involve you and Jim. By the way, where the hell is he? Did you say he was in San Juan?"

"Yes. He left early this morning on business."

"Well, hell. Listen, if I could maybe borrow a pair of his pants and a shirt, I could get out of here."

She said, "Tell me what has happened?"

He stared a moment longer out the window, seeing nothing. Finally he turned around on the couch and sat back. "Well," he said, "I just had a couple of unhappy customers. When we went to get on the plane this morning, I found out that they'd lied to me about the kind of job I was hired to do. I told them to get lost. They didn't like that, so they pulled out a pistol and I got the hell away from them." He shrugged. "That's about it."

"But surely not. How have you come to be running around in your birthday suit?"

He said, "Well, they decided to pay me a little visit awhile ago. I heard them as soon as they came into the room. I was out of there like a bolt of greased lightening. Just jumped off the balcony. Second story."

"Oh, my God!" She put her hand to her heart. Her robe had slipped and he could see the plump shape of her breasts under her nightgown. "You jumped from the second floor? From that hotel across the street?"

"Yeah. A pretty good drop."

"Are you hurt? Let me see."

He said, "I hurt my foot." He held it out. "Feels like the arch." He was grimacing. "Hope to hell it isn't broken."

She fell down to her knees and took his foot in her hands. "Oh," she said, "it is swollen. Ice is what is needed. And quickly."

She got up and went into the little kitchen of the trailer house. "I will get some ice cubes," she said.

"Listen, don't go to any trouble. I feel bad about busting in on you like this."

He heard her in the refrigerator. After a moment she was back with a large bowl full of ice cubes and water. "Here," she said. "We will put your foot in this."

She took his foot in her hands and guided it into the bowl. "Damn," he said, "that's pretty cold."

"Does it feel broken? What do you think?"

He shook his head. "I don't think I could have run on it if it were broken. Though my adrenalin level was pretty high. I think it's just sprained." He finished the last of the brandy in his glass and held it out to her.

"Would you like some more?"

"Yeah," he said, "I guess I would. And how are the cigarettes holding out?"

"There are plenty," she said. "There is plenty of everything."

He sat there, soaking his foot, while she got him another glass of brandy and lit a cigarette for him. He said, "Well, I damn well can't complain about the service. You better look out, you're liable to get me spoiled."

She was sitting on the couch beside him, her head turned, looking at him. She'd let the robe come completely loose in the front and the nightgown did little to hide her breasts. He was trying not to look, but he could see the points of her nipples pushing against the flimsy material of her nightgown. He could see that they were hard and he wondered if it was the coolness of the trailer with the air conditioner going. He'd let the sheet fall down from around his shoulders, just keeping it wrapped around his waist. She put her hand suddenly on his chest. She said, "You have a very nice chest." She rubbed her hand back and forth. "The hair on your chest is very soft, almost like fur. It feels good."

It took him so by surprise that he didn't quite know

what to say. He finally said, "Well, yeah, I guess so. But I ain't much of an expert on the hair on men's chests."

She continued rubbing his chest and then her hand slid down to his belly. "And such a flat stomach. You were an athlete?"

"Well, yeah," he said. "Sort of." He was talking rapidly. He was beginning to get embarrassed. He said, "I played a little college football. Smalltime stuff. Ran a little track. But mostly I rodeoed."

She moved her hand down further, stroking him gently.

He moved a little. "Olga," he said, "that kind of tickles. I'm ticklish as hell."

"No," she said calmly, "it doesn't tickle. You are becoming self-conscious, shy."

He laughed without much humor and took a drink of brandy. "Well, yeah, I guess I am. I don't quite know what to think about this."

Her hand moved further down, and he squirmed, trying to pull away. He said, "Listen, Olga, this ain't right. I don't come into a man's house and make out with his wife. That's against my code."

She said, with a quick little laugh, "I am not married to Jim. Did you think he was my husband?"

"Well, no," he said, feeling foolish. "But you're his woman. It's the same thing. He's been nothing but friendly to me and I'm not going to shit on him by doing something with his woman when he's gone. Especially not in his own house!"

She laughed out loud. "So that is what is troubling you. Your sense of honor, your code as you call it. Well, Jim is not my lover. We are friends. And we live together for convenience. Sometimes we make love together, but it is so much like incest that we both feel strange. At this moment he is with one of his girls in San Juan. I will tell him about your attitude. He will find that very humorous."

He said, "You're putting me on. You're joking."

"No," she said, "I am not. So, young man, you can forget your code. Unless you don't find me desirable."

He said, "Well, that ain't the case at all." She was still stroking his pubic hairs. He was starting to get very hard. He said, "Listen, just let me have another glass of brandy."

"Of course," she said, getting up. "There is no hurry. Your foot should soak at least a half an hour. I'm a registered nurse, even though I no longer work as one. And I haven't forgotten."

"You were a nurse?"

"Yes, for many years. That's how I happened to come to Puerto Rico, to work in a hospital in San Juan. They were paying very high salaries, much more than I could get in Dresden. I'm from Germany, you know."

"I kind of guessed that," he said. She brought him the glass of brandy. He said, "Well, didn't you like nursing better than running a cafe?"

"Oh no," she said. "Not at all." She sat back down beside him and began rubbing his chest and stomach again. "I like beautiful men's bodies and, as a nurse, most of the bodies I treated were sick or old. I didn't want to spend my life looking at wrinkles and wasted muscles." She pulled the sheet back and put her hand on his penis and began massaging it. She said, "Oh, so hard, and so nice and big."

"Gawd, Olga," he said. He took a quick drink of brandy. "Are you sure you're being straight with me about you and Jim?"

She didn't answer him, just slipped off the couch and knelt at his feet. She took him in her mouth. He reared his head back and clenched his teeth. "Oh hell!" he said. "Oh Christ!"

He put his glass of brandy on the floor and took his foot out of the bowl of water. Then he pushed her back on the floor by her shoulders, pulling up her nightgown as he did. She opened her legs to take him inside herself.

It was over very quickly. She was so slick and warm and soft and he was so aroused that it only took a moment. When he could talk, he said, "Damn, I'm sorry, babe. You didn't get much out of that. But blame yourself. You shouldn't have had me at the fever pitch."

She patted his head and stroked his hair. "No, I loved it. I loved feeling you spurting inside me. I have had a beautiful man."

He rolled off her and lay on his back on the floor. "Well, this beautiful man is worn out. Between you and the bad guys I'm about done in. This has been an eventful evening."

"Yes," she said. "Now you must sleep." She got to her feet and held her hand out. "Here, come on. I will take you to bed."

He let her help him up, still fearful of putting too much weight on his foot. She said, "It will feel much better tomorrow. If it doesn't, I will give you an injection of novacaine so that it will not bother you."

He said, "Florence Nightingale couldn't have been as good as you."

She led him into the tiny bedroom and helped him into bed. "Good night, Olga," he said, as she put the covers over him. She leaned down and kissed him lightly on the lips.

"Now you sleep."

"Yeah, I will. But I got to be up early."

"Don't worry," she said. "I will awaken you."

He was so tired all he wanted to do was pass out, but thoughts of Bonnie came into his mind. It made him angry. He was damned if he was going to feel guilty about her. Hell, she knew the score; she knew the rules. He'd never promised her he was going to be her man and hers alone.

He raised his head and punched at the pillow. "God-dammit," he said.

In the dark, from her side of the bed, Olga said: "Yes? Is something wrong?"

"No," he said. "Nothing at all. Just a little pain, but it will go away."

He awoke in the morning with the small bedroom flooded with sunlight. Olga was up, pulling open the blinds over the little windows. "Hi," he said. She was wearing her robe over her nightgown.

She looked around and smiled at him. "Good morning, sleepy head."

"How do you say good morning in German?"

"_Guten morgen._"

He said, "Do you know that it's almost impossible to say good morning in Spanish? You have to say, _bueno a las mañana_. You can say good afternoon or good night or good day pretty easily, but it's hell to say good morning. Apparently the Spanish aren't what you'd call morning people."

"Will you eat breakfast?"

"My favorite meal," he said. "But no coffee. I drink cold things in the mornings. Coke if you got it."

She said, "That is very strange. I have known one other man like that. He was an aerialist in the Circus Germany. A trapeze artist. Perhaps daredevils do not like coffee."

"Throws your timing off," he said. He yawned and threw the covers back and sat up. "Can I borrow your toothbrush? Yours, now, not old Jungle Jims. Using another man's toothbrush is a little too close to homosexuality to suit me."

She laughed. "Yes, of course." She pointed. "The

bathroom is just there. My toothbrush is the pink one. I will fix your breakfast.''

He took a shower and brushed his teeth. Then he looked in the closet and found a pair of Jim's pants. But they were too small. He finally decided the hell with it and went into the kitchen as naked as when he'd arrived. He said, ''Listen, I hate to keep walking around like this, but I haven't got anything to wear and I feel like an Arab with a sheet wrapped around me.''

''Do not concern yourself,'' she said. ''I'm going to dress in a moment and go to your hotel and get your belongings. Then you will have your clothes.''

He sat down at the table. ''Listen, I'm not sure if I want you to take that risk. Maybe you could just go out and buy me a pair of pants and a shirt. Then I could go over to the hotel.''

She was finishing up at the stove. ''No,'' she said, ''there is no reason for you to do that. Those men may be watching.''

''Well, what about you?''

She said, ''It will be very simple. I know the clerks at the hotel you are staying at. I will obtain a key to your room and go up. If someone is there, waiting for you, I will act surprised, as if I had the wrong room. If no one is there, I will gather up your belongings. But I will not come straight back here. I will park my little car in front of the hotel and drive off in that. If someone is watching, they will not see me come back here.''

''I'm impressed,'' he said. ''You Germans are very thorough.''

''Yes,'' she said. She put a plate of eggs and sausage in front of him, along with a glass of iced cola. ''There. Eat your breakfast. I will bring the toast.''

She left a half an hour later. He watched her drive off and then got a bottle of beer out of the refrigerator and sat in front of the little side window and watched the hotel. She pulled up some five minutes later, obviously having driven around a little, and parked in front of the hotel and went in. He was most worried about his billfold and his revolver. He'd told her where he'd put them, in his boots, and he hoped they'd still be there. If his pistol was gone he'd just have to find a way to get another one. For what he had in mind, he was going to need a gun.

She was gone a very brief time, fifteen minutes at the most. He heard the car pull behind the trailer house and then the door opened and she came in. She was carrying his clothes bag and his flight kit. She said, "I am sorry if it seemed a long time to you. I had to pack your shaving articles. And then I had trouble getting your cowboy boots in the bag."

He said, "Was my gun and billfold still there?"

"Oh yes. Your room was quite undisturbed. Whoever visited you left in a great hurry. However, the hotel is upset. They do not understand your strange departures and reappearances. They have asked that you not come back to the hotel." She smiled slightly. "There is no charge for last night. However, there is a bullet hole in the glass doors that lead to the balcony. Yes, they are quite upset with you."

He took the bags from her and laid them on the couch. First he opened his clothes bag and took out his boots. He could feel the weight of the .357 in one of them. He said, "Damn, Olga, I could just kiss you."

"Then why don't you?"

"All right." She was standing at his side and he turned and gathered her up in his arms and kissed her long and affectionately. He pulled back and said, "Thank you. Thank you for all your help."

She said, "Is that all the gratitude I get? Just words?"

She curled her hand around his body. "You have a very nice ass."

"Now, Olga," he said, "don't start that. I got some serious business on my mind and I don't want to be distracted. And you are a very distracting woman." He turned away and pulled a pair of Levis and a shirt out of his bag, and began dressing. She sat down in a chair, watching him. She said, "I hate to see you dress. I hate to see you hiding that beautiful body."

He said, "I wish another lady was as outspoken as you are. Or maybe she doesn't have the same opinion." He said it knowing that he was apologizing to Bonnie, in his own way, for what had happened the night before with Olga. And it made him as mad as hell that he felt any need to apologize.

"Oh?" she said. "Your wife?"

He shook his head. "No. We're not married. It ain't real smart for a guy in my kind of business to marry. No, it's just a woman I love."

She laughed; her laughter was silvery and crystal. "So this morning you are conscience-stricken."

He glanced at her, blushing slightly. "To tell you the truth, I was conscience-stricken last night. But she don't own me. I've made that very clear. And I ain't a damn bit sorry about last night."

"Then why do you mention her? It must be bothering you."

He buttoned his jeans and then hooked his belt and picked up his shirt. "Don't be so damn smart," he said. "It's not real brilliant of a woman to read a man so easily. Men don't like it." He sat down and pulled on a pair of socks. Then he put his billfold in his hip pocket and stuck his revolver in his waistband. Then he began to pull on his boots. The left one went on very easily, but he could not get the right one on over his injured foot. Olga was watching him, seeing the pain on his face.

She said, "Jim has some moccasins. They would be easier."

He shook his head. "No. The boots have a good high arch in them. If I can just get it on, I think I'll walk much easier."

She said, "You're probably right. I will get some talcum powder and we will see if that doesn't help."

With the talcum powder and a little effort he finally got the boot on. He stood up and tentatively tested it. There was some pain, but he could walk almost normally. "I believe that ice last night did the trick. It's going to be sore for a little while, but I think I'll live."

She was standing, leaning against a kitchen counter. She motioned toward the gun in his belt. "What are you going to do with that?"

He said, "I'm going to persuade a couple of ol' boys that shooting at me is not the right thing to do. I'm going to go see them in their nest, so I reckon I ought to be ready. I like things even. They got a gun. I *know* that. So I think I ought to have one."

She said, "I hope you do not get into trouble."

He shrugged. "Babe, I'm in trouble already, and so far as I can tell, I won't be out of it until I find those two hombres and clean their clocks for them."

She held out a key. "Here. This is to the door of the trailer in case you need to get in here in a hurry. I am going to work in the cafe in a little while."

"Well, thanks," he said.

"Are you going to leave without coming back to say good-bye? Or do you know?"

He said, "I don't want to leave without saying good-bye, but I can't promise anything. I might get in a hell of a rush."

"I understand," she said. "If you have to leave, don't worry about the key."

He went over and gave her a soft kiss on the lips. "Anyway," he said, "I can tell you without fear of contradiction that you are one hell of a lady. Even if I don't see you again this time around, I'll be back. My work brings me back here fairly often. Now you tell old Jungle Jim I said hello and to keep a beer in the window for my return."

Walking toward the Palomar Hotel he decided that what he was going to do was very unprofessional and very ill-considered, but he didn't give a shit. He was angry— angry to the point where he knew he was not thinking his best. If he were thinking professionally, he'd find a way off the island, either get his plane fixed or get another one or take a commercial flight and go home and forget the whole thing. But he wasn't going to do that. He thought, I am going to teach those two taco terrorists that I do not like to have guns pulled on me. I do not like to have my airplane disabled, and I do not like to have my sleep interrupted.

Oh, he was angry, no mistake about it. He stopped before he went into the little hotel lobby and pulled out his shirt to cover the revolver he had stuck in his belt. He didn't want to put it in his boot, for he figured he might need it in a hurry.

There was one clerk at the little desk, a young Puerto Rican looking bored and sleepy. China went up to the desk and asked if a man named Cortez was registered there. The young man shook his head. "No, I do not believe we have a party by any such name. No, there is no Cortez staying here."

That didn't surprise China. He hadn't expected Cortez had given him his right name. He described Cortez and the girl and the other man. The desk clerk shrugged. "Who knows?'' he said. ''Perhaps they are registered here, but I'm not sure.''

China took his billfold out and laid a hundred-dollar bill on the counter. He kept it partially hidden with his hand. He said, ''Now, you think, my friend.'' The desk clerk was staring hard at the bill. ''Yes,'' China said, ''this is going to be yours if you can remember who I am talking about and what room they're in.'' He described Cortez and his party again.

The young man said, ''And you are going to give me that hundred dollars if I tell you their room number?''

''Indeed I am,'' China said. ''And no questions asked.''

The young man glanced at a door just to the left of the desk. China figured it led to the switchboard. The desk clerk eyed the money and unconsciously smoothed his hair back. He said, ''I suppose it would do no harm. Are you a friend?''

''Oh yes,'' China said. ''I want to give them a little surprise. We are very good friends.''

''In that case I can see no harm.'' The clerk put his hand on top of the desk, very near the money. He said, ''They are in room 212.'' He moved his hand, palm upwards, closer to the money.

China said, ''All I need is a key and this hundred is all yours.''

''A key?'' The clerk looked uncertain. ''That is not good policy for the hotel, señor. To give out a key. Perhaps you could just knock. If they are such good friends. . . .'' He let his voice trail off.

China said, ''I really want to surprise them. I tell you what. You just leave the key lying on the end of the desk. Then you take this hundred dollars and turn your back. That way you won't have given me the key. I'll have taken it''

''Yes,'' the clerk said slowly, ''we could do that. I can

see no harm." He turned to the pigeonholes behind him and took out the key to room 212 and laid it on the end of the counter. "I know nothing of this," he said.

"A smart boy," China said. "You'll go far." He took his hand off the bill and flicked it with his forefinger so that it slid across the desk and disappeared over the edge. "Found money," China said. "Just lying there on the floor." He picked up the key as the clerk bent to pick up the money and then turned and went to the stairs that led toward the second floor.

Climbing the stairs his foot hurt a little, but the good solid arch in his boot was giving it enough support so that it was easily bearable.

He reached the landing and then began checking numbers. Room 212 was the last room at the end of the hall. A corner room. It was probably big. Maybe a suite. All three of them were staying there, so they'd had to have plenty of beds, unless the girl was sleeping with one of them. He doubted that. The girl was maybe being brought along against her will. He didn't know what their deal was, but he was damn well about to find out.

He pulled the revolver out of his belt and stood there with the key in his hand, running through his mind all that could happen and what he wanted to do about it when he went in the door. Surprise was going to be on his side. There would possibly be a chain lock on the door, but he could break that quickly with his shoulder and be inside the room, gun drawn, before they could react. His problem was that he didn't know his adversaries or what they were up to. It was best, then, to treat them as the worst people he'd ever known. He'd figure out how to deal with them once he had them in a captive position.

He put the key in the door as gently as he could and turned it. He felt rather than heard the lock click back. Then he turned the knob gently. The door opened. He

pushed it back, waiting for the stop at the end of the chain
lock. It didn't come. The door swung open a foot, then
two feet. There was no chain lock. He shoved the gun out
at the end of his arm and burst through the door, going to
his knees as he entered the room. He couldn't see anyone.
The bathroom was to his left, the door open. Still on his
knees he pushed the door wide and looked inside. The
room was empty.

"Hell," he said. He got to his feet and walked into the
big bedroom. The girl was lying on one of the beds, her
wrists and feet taped together and a band of adhesive tape
across her mouth. She turned her head and stared at him
with frightened eyes. There was no one else in the room.

He said, "Well, I'll be damned. Look what I found."

He walked up to the bed. Her eyes were very frightened.
He transferred the gun to his left hand and reached down
and peeled off the tape.

She gasped for breath for a second and then seemed to
shrink back from him. "Don't hurt me," she said. "Please
don't hurt me."

He was astonished. He said, "Hell, I ain't going to hurt
you. Don't you remember me? I was the pilot who wouldn't
let you on the plane yesterday morning."

Chapter Nine

It took her a moment. Her eyes looked much less cloudy than they had the day before. She didn't look as doped or as drunk. She stared at him, blinked her eyes and then said, "Oh yes, now I remember. Please help me! Please, please, they are killers."

"Just one second," he said. He turned and went swiftly to the door, shut it, locked it and put the chain lock on. There was no telling when the two men might return.

Then he went back to the bed and began peeling the tape off the girl. It hurt her coming off, but she didn't cry out. In a moment he had her free. She sat up on the side of the bed, looking dazed. She said, "Oh my God, I am so afraid. If I told you what they were going to make me do!"

He said, "Later. Right now we got to get out of here in a hurry, before someone comes knocking on the door. Get up and start trying to walk. Get some circulation going again.''

He picked her up by the arm and got her to her feet. She stumbled a little at first, but then he saw that she could make it on her own. He said, "Where are they? When are they coming back?''

She said, "They are out trying to find you. They are afraid of you. They want to kill you. They—''

He said, "That's all I want to hear. Let's you and I get the hell out of here. We can talk later.'' He pulled her by the arm. "C'mon, let's go.''

She suddenly stopped and pulled back. She stood there in the center of the room staring at him. She looked very young and very beautiful, even as rumpled as she was, and very frightened. She said, "No. Why should I go with you? I don't know who you are. Maybe you're just as bad as they are.''

He turned around and looked at her. He said, "Well, lady, that goes two ways. I don't know who you are either. I have seen you once before, doped to the eyes or drunk as hell. Now I find you taped hand and foot. I don't know who you are or who your two friends are or what you are all up to. All I know is those two misguided individuals tried to kill me. And I aim to convince them that that's not such a good idea. You come or stay, but there's no way I'm going to hang out in this room.''

She looked uncertain. She said, "You are not with them? Are you not their pilot?''

"Lady,'' he said, "you just told me yourself they were out looking for me. I'm a venture pilot, an independent operator who was hired by those two friends of yours. They harmed my airplane and they tried to shoot me. I do not exactly like them. But I don't know anything about you. For all I know, you are in with them up to your eyebrows. You stay here if you want to. I'm leaving.''

"Please," she said, a helpless sound in her voice. "Please, no, I'm sorry. Please help me."

"Listen, young lady, I ain't the Red Cross or the Salvation Army. I have to get moving. I don't want to get penned up in this room."

She said, "I have a small suitcase. Let me go with you. I will tell you about them. If you are the pilot of the plane, they are trying to kill you. I am very afraid."

He looked up at the ceiling. "Lady, get your goddam suitcase and let's *go!*"

He watched as she went to the side of the room and closed and locked a small valise that was on a stand there. He watched her to make sure she didn't come out with a gun. When she was ready, he said, "All right, you get in front of me. We're going down the stairs and then out the front door of the hotel. After that I don't know. And I can't imagine why I'm taking you with me. I got all the baggage I need."

He unlocked the door, took off the chain lock, and let her step into the hall in front of him. Then they walked toward the stairs. He had the revolver in his hand. She was carrying her suitcase.

At the stairs he indicated she should precede him and she went down until they reached the main floor. They went by the desk. He had put the revolver back in his belt. The clerk glanced up, but then quickly looked back down at the paper he was reading.

They went out the door and he said, "Turn right."

They walked a half a block down the street and then he stopped her. He said, "Let me think a minute."

He stood there, looking around in the hot sunshine. There were a few cars going down the narrow, potholed streets, and off in the distance he could see the harbor with the masts of the sailboats rising up. He thought for a long moment. Then he looked at her. She was wearing a linen suit with a short jacket. It went very well with her dark looks. She was, he thought, a very pretty girl, but that really had nothing to do with anything. He said, "Now listen, I got a safe place we can go to. Do you know what these guys are up to?"

"Oh yes," she said.

"You going to tell me about it?"

"Of course."

He thought a few seconds more. "All right. We'll go to this place I have in mind. Then you tell me everything you know. But my main purpose is to get the hell out of here and go back to Texas. I ain't really interested in anything else. I get more chances at this kind of foolhardiness than I want and I been to two goat ropings and a county fair, so I'm pretty hard to impress. What I'm trying to tell you is, if you want to go along with me, I'll take you out of here. If you really deserve to get out."

She said, "Just help me. Please."

She stood there, looking so helpless he could only say, "All right. Come along. But walk in front of me."

They went the three blocks to Jungle Jim's trailer and then cut across the grass behind the cafe. He had been looking the whole way, but he hadn't seen Cortez or his partner or anything that looked like a threat. At the trailer door he looked around before he unlocked the door and motioned the girl inside.

She went in and he followed, shutting the door quickly. The trailer was empty. He pointed at the couch by the front wall. He said, "Sit down there. I got to think and we got to talk, but don't say anything for a few minutes."

She was looking around the trailer. "Whose place is this?"

He said, "I told you to shut up for a minute." He went to the refrigerator, got out a bottle of beer, lit a cigarette and sat down in a chair opposite her. For a moment he just sat there smoking and looking at her, trying to figure what she was all about. Finally he said, "What's your name?"

"Ugette."

"Where you from?"

"Columbia. From Bogata, Columbia."

"Yeah?" He drew on his cigarette and looked at her. "You don't look South American to me. You don't even look Latin."

"I'm not," she said. "My mother was French and my father was an American oil geologist. They met in Columbia and I was born there."

"You still live there?"

"Yes."

He jerked his head. "That where you met your two boy friends? The two that don't know how to act in civilized society?"

She looked down at her hands. Without looking up she said, "They are not my friends, believe me."

"Then who are they? Are they Columbians also?"

"Yes, I think so." But there seemed to him to be a hesitancy in her voice.

He drained his beer bottle and got up and got another one. He said as he sat back down, "Girl, you better not start lying to me. Not if you want me to get you out of this town. What do you mean, you *think* they're Columbians?"

She said, "I—I have not known them very long. Or very well. They came to me. They knew about me."

"And what did they come to you about?"

She looked down at her hands again and drew her legs up, seeming to be drawing inside herself. She didn't answer and he said, "Well? What did they come to see you about?"

She finally answered in a low voice. She said, "It is a very shameful thing I was going to do. I am ashamed to speak of it. But I can tell you they are very bad men."

He said, "Oh shit, girl! That ain't going to get it. I don't need you to tell me they're bad men. All I need you to do is tell me what they were up to. And I ain't going to pull it out of you by bits and pieces. If you don't tell me, and damn quick, I'm leaving you right here."

She looked up, "No! Please! They would kill me for certain."

"Then you better tell me. I've got to know what I'm up against. And I mean it. I haven't got much time."

She looked down again. He waited and, after a moment, she began to talk. "They are international terrorists. At first, when I agreed to do the shameful thing, I did not know how awful they were. I was hurt and angry and I didn't realize what I was getting into. I was just very angry at the man and I wanted very much to pay him back for what he'd done to me."

He said impatiently, "What man? Who are you talking about?"

Still without looking up, she said, "My lover. In Columbia. He was the chief operating officer in Columbia for a large American oil company that had very big holdings in South America. Of course, you know that the terrorists have kidnapped many industrial executives and held them for large ransoms to embarrass the capitalist countries and to finance their political activities."

He was rapidly beginning to get the picture. He said, "And your boy, your lover, was going to be one of the targets?"

"Yes. Only I didn't know that then. He left; he was recalled back to the United States before he could be kidnapped."

"To Georgia? To Atlanta?"

She looked up. "Yes. How did you know that "

"Hell, they the same as told me. But I thought they were going to rob a bank or pick up a load of drugs. I was way off the mark. Were they going to kidnap your lover in the United States? Was that the game?''

"Yes. They wanted to prove that nobody was safe from them anywhere. They were going to take him to Nicaragua, I believe, and hold him there.''

China said slowly, "So he was going to be my fourth passenger. Your old lover.'' Then he looked up at her. "But what was going to be your part in this scheme? Where did you come in? You're not a terrorist, are you?''

"No,'' she said quickly. "Of course not. I have no politics. I'm not interested in politics.'' She looked away from him. "Only in getting married and having a family.''

He said, "Then what were you supposed to do?''

She was still looking away from him.

"Tell me,'' he said. "Dammit!''

She said, "I was to be the bait, the lure—to draw him to a place he could be safely abducted.''

"You what!'' He was surprised in spite of himself. This sweet, innocent-looking young girl was going to do something like that? "The hell you say!''

"Yes, I was,'' she said. There was a little break in her voice. "Or I was at first. Then I changed my mind.''

"But what the hell had this guy done to you that you'd set him up like that? You said he was your lover. The only female that treats a lover like that is a black widow spider. Hells bells, lady!''

She turned her head back toward him and for just a second he could see the spark of anger in her eyes. She said, "He promised to marry me! He was going to divorce his wife in America and marry me! He promised me that for two years. When he was transferred back to America, I would go with him.''

China laughed dryly. "How old are you, little girl? Twenty-four? Twenty-five?''

"I am twenty-five," she said. "What difference does that make?"

"Because you sound about eighteen, talking like that. I guess you think you were the first girl ever got fed that old song and dance." He made a sound of disgust.

"But it hurt me very bad," she said. "John, that's his name, had been promising me what I would have in the United States—the big house, the servants. We would even keep his children and then have some of our own. He promised me, for two years! We were so much in love I could never doubt him."

China drew on his cigarette and gave her a cynical look. "And then he got called home and he was sorry, baby, but there just wasn't room for you. Something like that?"

She nodded quickly and put her hand to her mouth as if she was going to cry.

China got up and went to the refrigerator. He said, "If you start crying, you're going to do it on your own time. Because I'll be gone."

He opened the beer, took a quick look out the front window and then sat back down opposite her. He said, "And so these two baboons came to you with the proposition of how you could get back at him for the great hurt he'd done you."

She nodded quickly, still with her hand at her mouth.

"But how'd they find you?"

"Our affair was well-known. You could not know about him without knowing about me. He had an apartment for appearance's sake, but he really lived in the apartment he had bought me." She suddenly leaned toward China. "But I swear, on my mother's head, I didn't know they would really hurt him. They said they would just scare him a little and that I could have the satisfaction of making him believe that I'd been the one who'd done it."

China laughed dryly.

"No, I swear it. Look, I know you don't know me, but I'm not bad. Not that bad. It was only later that I understood they'd been lying to me. And that was only after we'd left Columbia and come here. Then I tried to leave, when I found out truly who they were—what they were really like. I didn't want to see John really hurt, I swear it!"

China regarded her over the end of his cigarette.

She repeated emphatically, "I tried to leave. I told them I knew their plans and I wanted no part of them. I was going to warn John. That's when they doped me. That was what was the matter with me the morning they brought me to your plane. I was so groggy I couldn't see straight. But they were still going to make me talk to John on the phone, lure him some way, even if only to save my own life." She suddenly began to cry softly. "I'm so afraid."

He got up and walked over and looked out the window again. There was still no one in sight. He patted her clumsily on the head. He said, "Well, Ugette, I guess you got a right to cry. And you're not really eighteen, like I said; you're more like fifteen. If you ever want to buy any beach-front property in Kansas, I got some for sale. But I guess if I'd been through what you been through, I might be crying too." He stared out the window a moment more. Then he said, "You sit there quiet. I got to think what to do."

After a few minutes he got up and went to the door. "Ugette, I'm going out for a little while. Maybe a couple of hours."

She got a suddenly more fearful look on her face. "You're not going to leave me! I'm terrified of being stranded here."

"Don't worry," he said, "I'm not going to leave you."

He patted the hand that she stretched out toward him. "I've got to go and figure out how to get us out of this mess. And the only way I can do that is to go out to the airport and have a little look around."

Her face got alarmed. She said, "But what will happen to me if something happens to you!"

He gave her an amazed look and said, "I'll tell you, little girl, if something happens to me, I doubt if I'll give a flying fuck in hell what happens to you. I didn't take you to raise."

He took another moment to explain about the cafe and the trailer house and who they belonged to. He said, "Now you lock this door after I'm gone and don't unlock it except for the lady I told you about or for Jungle Jim. But from what I heard, I don't think he'll be back today."

He stepped outside the door, waited until he heard her lock it, then walked the little distance over to the cafe. There was a screen door at the back and from the smells coming out, he could tell it led to the kitchen. He opened it and stepped inside. Olga stood at the stove with her back to him, busy with something she was frying on the grill. China didn't see anyone else in the kitchen. It was just a little after noon, so he figured she had a heavy lunch crowd. He let the screen door come to with a slight bang and said, "Hi."

She looked around, frowning. She was wearing a full-length cook's apron and had her hair done up in a kerchief. She looked the perfect house frau, frowning at the interruption and wiping at the sweat on her forehead with the back of her hand. Then she saw China and smiled. She said, "Ah, you did not go after all. Have you come for some lunch? Good, you can keep me company in the kitchen. Sit down at that little table."

"No," China said, "I'm a little pressed for time, Olga."

He went up and looked over her shoulder. She was frying chicken fried steaks. He said, "You know you have to be a Texan to make a good chicken fried steak."

"Fah!" she said. "I can cook anything. You sit down and try one."

He said, "Babe, I still got problems on my hands. I've got to go straight out to the airport and check on the condition of my airplane. Things have gotten even more complicated."

As simply as he could, without going into too many details, he explained about the girl and the god damn hole she'd dug herself into. He did not explain what the two terrorists were planning, only that the girl's life would be in danger if they found her. As he talked, Olga's eyes widened.

When he was finished, she immediately said, "You must go to the police. Call them on the telephone in the corner."

He shook his head. "No, Olga, reckon not. It's our policy not to get mixed up with the police at all, if we can help it. And then only police we have some sort of understanding with. They ask too many questions that we don't like to answer."

She said, "Then wait until Jim gets back. He should be here tonight. Let him help you; don't try it alone."

He half smiled. "Well, no," he said, "I don't think I'll do that either. But I appreciate the offer. Anyway, I've probably got the wind up for no good reason at all. I bet these guys have already left Fujardo and are a hundred miles away from here by now. I just wanted to check with you and make sure it'd be all right to leave the girl there while I'm gone."

Olga said, "Of course it's all right. But why don't you take my car instead of using a cab?"

He shook his head. "Don't want those boys to connect me with this place. Anyway, I'll see you in a little while."

She smiled slightly. "How's the foot?"

"It's pretty good," he said. Then he laughed. "I got my big gun in the other boot so the limping about balances out. I just look like I'm drunk, or a sailor. Maybe both."

She said, "Now you be careful."

"Sure," he said, thinking she sounded like Bonnie. "See you later."

He went out the door and angled away from the cafe, cutting over two small side streets before coming back up to the main street to catch a taxi. He saw no sign of Cortez or his cohort.

Riding out to the airport, he thought over all the contingencies and what he intended to do about each. He also eased the revolver out of his boot and stuck it under his shirt, deep inside his waistband. He'd killed before, and not just with the impersonal guns of a fighter plane. He hadn't liked it before and he didn't expect he'd ever like it. But he was feeling that cold, stonewall feeling he got when someone had pushed him too far and he wasn't going to be pushed any farther. He didn't really want any more trouble, even though, in truth, he was liking Cortez and his partner less and less the more he knew about them.

But, he reminded himself, your job is to fly the airplane. Leave the righting of wrongs and the justing of injustice to the do-good boys. Your only crusade is the well-being of you and yours, even though that seems to be slipping your mind a lot lately.

Still he wasn't sure if he wanted Cortez and his fellow goon to cross his path again or not. He kind of halfway hoped they would, even though it was against his better judgement. He knew what terrorists were, and he didn't much like such people. As a matter of course, he didn't like anyone who set himself up to instruct anyone, unasked, on anything. Especially if that instruction required bombing, torture, kidnapping, shooting, or any other form of mayhem deemed necessary to get the subject's attention.

But, as he kept reminding himself, China, you are just a dumb country boy. Don't presume to understand the way such great minds work.

Anyway, he had enough problems of his own.

At the airport he had the driver pull up at the entrance just off the main road. The beach was just opposite the landing strip, separated from it only by the road. There were bathers there, and people just taking the sun—nothing to make him suspicious. Finally he turned and walked down the little oyster-shell entrance road to the airport, going the hundred or so yards to the flight service station with the hangar next door. He looked in the window of the ready room shack but saw only the clerk dozing behind the counter. Then he went on around and found the mechanic at the back of the cavernous hangar, working on the engine of a Cessna 182. China went up to him. "Hi. Get my magneto cable in?"

The mechanic stopped and wiped his hands on some waste. "Yeah, got 'em in this morning. Kept waiting for you to call." He took time to spit tobacco juice at a nearby can, partially hitting it. "I went ahead and installed the part. Would have run the engine up to check if it was all right, but you didn't leave me the key."

"That's all right," China said, thinking the mechanic hadn't needed the key. Most airplane keys were interchangeable. He himself had keys to most of the standard Pipers and Cessnas in his own pocket. But he said, "I ain't too worried about it running. Let me pay you and get squared away here at the airport."

The mechanic said, "Let's go to the office and I'll make you out a ticket."

They went into the office and the mechanic got behind the counter, shoving the clerk out of the way while he wrote up China's bill. When he was through, China paid him and then paid the clerk for the tie-down fee and the gas they'd put in his plane. As he and the mechanic were walking out, China asked, casually, if the mechanic had seen anyone around his airplane.

The mechanic spit on the ground. He said, "Hell, buddy, there's people running around all over this airport every day. People walk by your airplane going to theirs and by yours coming from theirs. You got anybody special in mind?"

China described Cortez and his partner. The mechanic looked at him and laughed. He said, "You're in Puerto Rico, buddy. Take a good look around you. Them two gents you just described ain't exactly going to stick out in this crowd, are they?"

China smiled ruefully. "Yeah. I see what you mean."

The mechanic was looking at him. "Did they have anything to do with what happened to that magneto cable?"

"No," China lied. "Not that I know of. Well, much obliged for your work. I won't be taking off right now, but if I ever need any help this way, I'll come to you."

He left the hangar and walked toward the flight line. He did not go all the way to his airplane, but he got near enough so that he could see that no one was around it. If they were lurking somewhere out of sight, he didn't want to alert them until the last possible moment. By now they would know the girl was gone and they'd probably guess that he'd found her and taken her somewhere. The desk clerk at their hotel, hundred dollars or no hundred dollars, could be counted upon to give them that information. His best bet would be just to arrive at the field as suddenly and as swiftly as possible, jam the girl in the plane, and be wheels-up before they knew what had happened.

He got a cab and went back to the trailer, having the driver stop a full block away. He thought of checking in with Olga at the cafe, but then decided that he'd see how the girl was doing first. He'd been gone better than two hours and he figured she was probably scared out of her wits.

He knocked gently on the door and then waited, expecting a voice from within immediately. There was no sound. He knocked again, a little harder, and waited. Nothing happened. Dammit, he thought, is the woman deaf? He knocked again, harder still. Maybe, he thought, she was in the bathroom. While he was trying to find the key Olga had given him, he tried the knob. It opened and the door swung back.

"Oh shit!" he said softly. He pushed the door all the way back and then waited. Nothing happened. He stuck his head just inside the sill and took a quick look around. The interior of the trailer looked empty.

He waited another moment, then pulled the .357 out of his belt, cocked it and went swiftly through the door. There was not a sound in the trailer.

Swiftly he checked the only other two rooms, the bedroom and the bathroom. They were empty. The girl was not there. He came back into the living room and slumped down in a chair. "I'm a son-of-a-bitch!" he said aloud. She had left on her own after he'd told her not to. There wasn't the slightest sign of a struggle or of a window or door being forced. Even her suitcase was still sitting where she'd set it by the small couch. The little fool had walked right out the door and probably got herself caught the first rattle out of the box.

He sat a moment, smoking a cigarette, the .357 limp in his hand. Finally he thought: To hell with her. I did not take her to raise. I am going to go tell Olga good-bye and get myself out to that airport and go home to Texas. I am not going to spend my time looking for some harebrained girl in this town. He got up, collected his bags, let himself out of the trailer, locked the door behind him and walked over to the back door of the cafe.

Chapter Ten

She was sitting at the table in the kitchen, drinking coffee with Olga. They both looked up as he came through the screen door. He let it slam behind him as he set his bags down. "Well, hello," he said to Ugette. "I figured you'd left town." He did not say this too nicely.

Olga said, "Now, China, don't be angry with her. I thought she would be afraid over there by herself, so I brought her here to wait with me. I thought it would be safer."

China smiled sourly. "And also get you more involved. Which I was trying to avoid." He looked at the girl, hard. "I like my orders obeyed. I'm used to it. It makes me very nervous when they are not."

The girl looked down. "I'm sorry. I didn't know what to do."

Olga patted a chair beside her. "Sit down, beautiful pilot. And have something to drink. We have time to visit. The cafe is almost empty."

193

China dropped into the chair. "I got time for a quick beer and a quick good-bye kiss. Then we got to be on our way. It looks clear right now, so I don't want to push my luck by wasting any time. Ugette here tells me she thinks they got friends in these parts, which leaves me not knowing who to look for."

Olga's face took on a troubled look. "China, I don't really know much about these men except they have shot at you and scared this poor girl to death. What are they, drug dealers?"

He shook his head. "No, much worse. Fanatics. Dangerous fanatics. Killer fanatics. Drug dealers only want to ruin the lives of a select few million people. These boys are after everyone. And how about that beer?"

She got up quickly and disappeared through the kitchen door that led into the bar and the dining room.

He looked at Ugette; she dropped her eyes. He said, "It's all right. But it might get worse. We need to get your suitcase out of the trailer. Why didn't you think to bring it?"

Olga was coming through the door. "The suitcase I will get," she said. She set his beer and a glass down in front of him. "You drink that and I will hurry across and be right back. And then you can be gone." She went out the door.

China poured beer in his glass and looked at Ugette. "The suitcase ain't important," he said. "Your leaving with Olga ain't important. What is important is that from now on you do exactly as I tell you until we get away from here. And you do it instantly. Do you understand that?"

She looked down at her hands. "Yes," she said.

He reached over and took her chin, forcing her face up so that she was looking at him. "No, not just a weak yes. You got to do better than that, babe. These are bad guys and my life might be on the line and I don't want to lose it because you hesitated when I said jump. I tell you to jump, you better jump without thinking. You got that?''

"Yes," she said, a little stronger.

"All right," he said. He sat back, drinking the beer and brooding over what a disaster his last two jobs had been. One wrecked airplane, no fee; one disabled airplane, half a fee. God, he thought, if he kept this pattern up much longer, he was going to begin owing the company money. But sometimes it was like that. And sometimes the flights were such milk runs that you felt a little guilty about taking the money.

Olga came through the back door and set the girl's suitcase down. China drank the last of his beer and stood up. He said, "Time to go, darlin'."

She looked distressed. "Why do you go? Why take the chance? Why not stay here a few days in our trailer until those men leave? They can't stay here forever. After that you could go with no risk."

"Sorry, honey," he said, "but that don't feed the bear. No, I got to get home and make a little money for bear feed before he eats us out of house and home and I find myself out in the cold." He went up to Olga and took her in his arms and gave her a long hug and then a brief kiss. "It goes without saying," he said, "how much I appreciate this." He got out his billfold and took out a card. It was blank except for the man in New York's phone number. He said, "You ever need me, you call this number and the people at that end will find me and I'll get back in touch with you."

He kissed Olga again and then he and the girl went out the back door, leaving her standing there watching him. It seemed to him like he was always leaving good people for not very good reasons.

He went three blocks this time before locating a cab. The girl had a difficult time walking in her high heels and carrying her bag. But China had his two bags in his left hand and he wanted his right free for the revolver he'd stuck back in his belt.

Riding out to the airport, the girl became apprehensive. She said, "Do you think they'll be there?"

He said, "If I were them, I'd be there."

"But why don't they just go away!" Her voice was strained. He didn't like the sound of it. She said, "Why don't they just leave and forget us. We mean no harm to them."

He shook his head. "They can't, babe. If we get away from them, they will have failed. And people like them can't fail. If the word gets around, it's liable to be their finish. First they fucked up with you; then they fucked up with me. And now we're about to fuck their main job up. We're a threat to them and they can't have that. Plus they think I got six thousand dollars of their money. I imagine that the first time they came after me, in my hotel room, it was to try to get their money back. But then I got you loose from them and I imagine they are about as mad as a wet settin' hen." He lit a cigarette. He wanted to reassure her as much as he could because he didn't like the spooked way she was sounding. But he also wanted her alert. "Those boys don't give two cents for your life, or mine, or even their own. They honest-to-God believe in what they're doing. That's what makes them so damn scary."

She said, her voice frightened, "Then let's go to the police. Now!"

He looked at her. "You can go to the police if you want to. As soon as I get out to the airport, you can turn this cab around and go straight to the police. That is, if you really want to."

"Why not? I've done nothing wrong."

He nodded. "Not legally, no. I agree. And in five or six

weeks you might succeed in convincing the police of that. But you've gotten yourself mixed up with some heavy-duty trouble-makers, and the police are going to think you know a whole lot more about them and their kind than you really do. And they are going to be awfully determined to find out just how much you do know.''

She said, ''You could go with me. They would believe both of us.''

He laughed dryly. ''Look, dolly, we've been over all that. This might be your last trip on the roller coaster, but it won't be mine. My bunch doesn't go to the police. The outfit I work with has got the same motto as the little bank back home I do business with—Safety, Service, Silence. Nearly all the clients we work for, usually with good reason, are kind of shy and retiring when it comes to the police. We go to getting our names on too many police blotters, for whatever reason, and it wouldn't be long before we'd be out of business.''

The cab was nearing the entrance to the airport. China leaned forward quickly and told the driver, ''Go ahead, but go slowly. I'll tell you when to stop.''

''*Si, señor*,'' the driver said.

China took ten dollars out of his billfold and handed it across the seat to the driver. He said, ''That will cover the fare. You keep the change. When we get out, we'll be getting out in a hurry. You understand?''

''*Muchas gracias. Si. Yo comprendo.*''

As they drove down the narrow shell road, he was watching carefully, but seeing nothing. There were about six rows of airplanes parked back on the grass from the landing strip. His was still in the front row. He did not want to approach it directly. Three rows from the front he told the driver sharply, ''Stop!''

As the cab came to a halt he was opening the door.

"Come on," he said to the girl. She was opening the door on her side. He said, "Here, dammit!"

"But it's easier over—"

"Goddammit!" He grabbed her arm and dragged her across the seat. "Move when I tell you!"

"Let me get my bag!"

He crouched, watching, as she pulled herself and her bag out of the cab. Then he led her along a row of airplanes, away from his. He wanted to approach his airplane from the opposite side. When he thought he'd gone far enough, about halfway down the row, he stopped and watched for a moment.

She said, "What is it?"

"Goddammit, shut up!" he hissed.

He waited another moment, then drew the revolver. Holding it in his right hand, he led them through the lines of aircraft up toward the flight line. They broke clear into the space between the first line and the second, a distance of some ten yards. He crouched under the nose of an Aeronica and looked carefully to the right. He could just see the tail assembly of his airplane. Nothing much else seemed to be going on—he could see a line boy casually tying down an airplane a few parking spaces back. He waited until the line boy was through and had gone away, and then he waited a moment more. In his mind he reviewed what needed to be done. His airplane was tied down under each wing, but they were chain tie-downs with quick snaps. He could have them off in an instant. After that it was shove the girl in, get in himself, and start taking off as soon as he had both engines started. There'd be no time for a preflight check. He'd have to risk it.

Maybe, though, he thought, they're not even here. Maybe they've done something else to the airplane and not to check it would be a bad mistake.

He crouched there, considering. Then he started getting

angry. He was getting damn good and tired of this foolishness. Dammit, they were going to walk on down to that airplane and he was going to cut the tie-downs, pull the checks, do a normal preflight and then take off as he ordinarily would.

He said to the girl, "C'mon, we're going."

With her behind him they started down the lane between the airplanes. They walked slowly. There was no movement, nothing in sight. As they walked, his mind turned back to a time in Viet Nam when there'd been a rumored infiltration of the airfield he was flying out of. Even at a supposedly secured air base they'd had to approach the airplane as gingerly as you would a time bomb. And then, after ten minutes of skulking up on the airplane, expecting mortar attacks or rockets or automatic fire from the surrounding jungles, nothing had happened. Sometimes false alarms in a combat zone freaked soldiers out as much as the real thing.

He said, the girl behind him, "We're almost there. Don't worry. I think everything's okay."

And there was the airplane. They walked up to it, coming into the V between the wing and the fuselage on the right side. He said, "Just stand right here. I'm going to release the airplane and do a few checks and I'll be right back."

He went to the port wing and released the tie-down, then did a walk-around check as he came to the starboard wing. The girl was watching him. He released the other tie-down. He looked at her over the top of the low wing and smiled. "It's all right. We're okay. We'll be gone in about two minutes."

Then he walked back around the tail of the airplane and checked the moveable surfaces of the elevators. She was standing there, looking back at him apprehensively. He checked the ailerons on the starboard wing. They seemed

fine. He did not check either engine. He came back around
to the V between the fuselage and the wing. He said,
"Everything looks okay. I believe we are going to get out
of here with the kitchen sink and all the parts we brought."
He stepped up on the wing and opened the cockpit door.
Everything inside looked like it was supposed to. He
turned to reach for Ugette, holding out his hand to help her
up on the step. At that instant he heard a sound. Not a
shout, not a yell, more the presence of a sound than a
sound expressed. He swiveled his head around. He saw
three men running down the open lane between the lines of
planes. They were perhaps twenty yards away. Cortez was
out in front. China could see the drawn pistols in their
hands. They stood out very dark and deadly against all the
other colors he was seeing. He stepped down from the
wing. With his right arm he shoved Ugette back. He said,
"Get down Now!"

Then he pulled the .357 out of his waistband and leveled
it down across the wing at the rushing men. He pulled the
hammer back with his thumb, hearing the *clitch clatch*
sound a revolver makes when you cock it. Cortez was still
in front, revolver in hand. He was wearing a light blue
shirt with dark blue buttons. China sighted on the second
button from the top of the shirt and squeezed off the shot.
The magnum revolver went loud in his hand and Cortez
suddenly stopped running and flipped over backwards.
Then the other two were firing. China heard a bullet crash
into the windscreen of the airplane and another hit the
wing and went singing off in the distance. He aimed a shot
at the man on the right, fired, turned without seeing if he'd
hit, then jerked Ugette around and started pushing her
away from the airplane. "Run!" he said. "Goddammit!
Run!"

He scooped up his flight kit with his left hand and
shoved her along with his right elbow. "*Move!*"

He led them across the open lane, running toward the second line of aircraft. She was limping behind him. He turned, running backwards. "C'mon, goddammit!"

She said, "My heels! My shoes, I can't run in them."

He shoved the revolver in his belt, grabbed her by the arm and jerked her under the wing of a Cessna 210. Then he turned and crouched there, looking for pursuit. He'd surprised them by his sudden gunfire attack and they were probably under cover. But that would be only for the moment. Just as he was, they were probably crouched under the wing of an airplane, looking for movement, trying to figure where he was. But they wouldn't wait long. Very shortly they'd be slipping through the lines of airplanes, trying to flush him out. And there were two of them, both with guns, and all he had was the handicap of a hysterical girl. She was clinging to his back, gasping and sobbing. He said, "Goddammit! Be quiet!"

He looked around, trying to think of what he could do. He was in a fix, and no mistake.

Then, far off, he heard the sound of a police siren. Oh shit, he thought. That's all we need. The goddam police.

Then he heard a familiar noise, the sound of an aircraft engine being started. He turned and looked over his shoulder. He could see nothing but the fuselage and tail assemblies of the aircraft in the front row. But, as he watched, he saw the vertical stabilizer of a yellow and white Cessna 172 begin to shake slightly. He couldn't see the propeller, but he knew that was the airplane that was being started. The plane was about twenty yards down. It would mean a dash across the open lane between the lines of aircraft.

He didn't hesitate. He got up, jerking the girl to her feet. "C'mon, and run like hell." Pulling her behind him, running low, he sprinted as fast as he could toward the tail of the yellow and white airplane. Halfway across he heard the sound of two shots and heard the bullets sing over their heads. Then another bullet smacked into the fuselage of an airplane right next to them. Then they were at the 172. China led them around the tail and came up to the cockpit on the pilot's side. The engine of the plane was ticking over slowly. China jerked the door open. A small, bespectacled man was sitting in the pilot's seat carefully studying a preflight list, oblivious to what had been going on around him. He looked around, startled, as China threw open the door. China said, "Set the emergency brake and get out—quick!"

"What?" the man exclaimed in astonishment.

China drew the .357 out of his belt and shoved it in the man's face. "Get out. I want your airplane. Move, dammit!"

The man was still too startled to react. China reached in, flipped the quick release of the safety belt the man was wearing, grabbed him by the shirt collar and dragged him out of the airplane. The man landed on the ground. He didn't seem hurt, but China had no time to check. Even at that instant he expected the two men to show up. He wondered distractedly, as he threw the pilot's back rest forward and grabbed the girl by the arm and shoved her in the back seat, where the third man had come from. As the girl had said, they obviously had contacts in Puerto Rico.

But he had no time to worry about that. He put his foot on the wing strut step. The man had turned and was sitting on the ground, looking astounded, his glasses askew on his nose. He said, "You can't steal my airplane!"

"I ain't," China said. "I'm just borrowing it. But there are men with guns coming. I advise you to get the hell out of here." He could hear the police sirens wailing louder. "Your plane will be all right," he said. Then he leaped into the cockpit and without pause, without bothering to shut the door, he pushed the throttle halfway in and started taxiing for the runway. As he approached the paved surface, intending to turn right, he saw the two men running toward him from that direction. "Oh shit!" he said. He revved the engine and pushed left rudder and turned in the other direction. But he was almost at the end of the field and there wasn't room to take off in the direction he was heading. Even above the engine he heard the sounds of the shots they were firing at him. All they had to do, he thought, was to hit a control surface and he might very likely be out of business. He crammed on more power, taxi-ing the airplane dangerously fast. The line of aircraft to his left was almost a blur.

There was only one way out—the highway. He'd have to get to it somehow, turn into the wind, pray there was no traffic, and somehow get the plane off in the little distance the curving road would give him.

He reached the end of the line of airplanes and turned left, slowing a little, but still taxiing much too fast for abrupt turns. He felt the plane tilt slightly over to the starboard wheel, felt the port wing come up. He thought: You may do the impossible, you may be fixing to ground loop a tricycle gear airplane.

But then the plane settled back and he taxied rapidly toward the beach highway at the edge of the field. As he neared, he pulled back power and got on the toe brakes, slowing the airplane. It looked as if he was going to be lucky. There was very little traffic. Using the throttle and the toe brakes he bumped over the rough ground separating the edge of the field from the highway. Then he threw in left rudder and started to turn left. As he did, he saw a police car start to turn in at the entrance to the airport and come to a skidding stop. They had obviously seen him. The police car backed up and then jumped back on the highway and started toward him. He could see two more police cars behind the first one.

"Shit!" he said.

There was only one place left to get the plane off. The

beach. He shoved the power forward, taxiing across the highway, then through the grass and onto the sand. He kept the power up, fearful the plane would stick in the loose drift sand. He turned the plane, aiming it down the beach. The waterfront was not crowded, but it was not empty either. The first of the bathers, some fifty yards ahead, stopped what they were doing and stared at him. To his left he could see the police cars come swerving off the highway, bumping over the rough ground, then throwing up rooster tails as they hit the loose sand.

He stood on the toe brakes and pushed the throttle all the way to the wall. The airplane strained and jerked, wanting to go. He ran the trim halfway back and then pulled the wheel back in to his belly, as far as it would go. He yelled aloud, "People, I hope you get my intentions and have the good sense to get out of the way because I'm coming through."

The first police car was only some twenty yards away when he released the toe brakes and the airplane instantly began to roll. Ahead of him the people began to run back from the beach. He was making a classic short field take off, hoping, praying, that the people would get out of the way.

He kept the airplane as close to the water's edge as he could. Behind him he could hear the girl whimpering quietly.

He really had more of a crosswind than a headwind. The wind was blowing in from the sea and he kept trying to point the airplane in that direction, edging it in as much as he could, hoping for the extra lift the wind would give him. He could feel the airplane beginning to lighten, but his ground speed was only up to forty knots and he needed at least ten more to even hope to get the airplane off the ground. The bathers were running away from the water's edge, leaving him a clear path, but ahead he could see a group clustered around a beach umbrella, oblivious to his rushing approach.

They were down near the water's edge, leaving him no place to go. He prayed silently: please look up. Please get your fucking heads out of your asses and get the hell out of the way!

The distance shortened. He could see they were gathered around a little table of some sort, eating a picnic lunch. He thought, wildly: it's too fucking late in the afternoon to be eating. You idiots! Look up! Please!

It was too late to cut power and hope to stop before hitting them. His only other option was to turn the plane to the right and drive it into the crashing breakers. The girl had started to scream.

Fuck it, he said silently. I'll make it fly before it's ready. He reached down to the lever between the seats and cranked in fifteen degrees of flap. The airplane slowed slightly, but he felt it lighten, now beginning to skip over the sand. The people were twenty yards ahead. He cranked in another fifteen degrees. With his left eye he could see the air-speed indicator. He was only making forty-five knots, but then, with a slight pressure on the right rudder pedal, as delicately as if there were a grape he didn't want to mash between his foot and the pedal, he turned the airplane slightly more into the wind blowing in from the sea. He felt the plane lift. Holding the wheel with his left hand, he sought for the delicate balance between stalling and flying. The airplane was off the ground. The umbrella, with its group of people, was just below. He raised the left wing ever so slightly and cleared the top of the umbrella with perhaps a foot to spare. As he flashed by, he had a quick impression of the upturned, horrified faces staring up at him.

He held the airplane in the right-wing-down attitude until he was by. The wing tip was in danger of catching the breakers that were rolling in. As delicately as he could, he brought the airplane back to the horizontal; his heart in his mouth, he expected, at any second, one of the landing gear wheels to catch a wave and send them plunging into the surf.

But it didn't happen, and gradually momentum and power began to catch up so that the airplane was flying by itself, without his will holding it up.

The air-speed indicator crept up to sixty and then sixty-five and then seventy and he was able to let the flaps off slowly. He began a slow right turn, still skimming the waves, on a heading that would take him to Miami.

He was free, he was flying.

He climbed to twenty feet above the waves and set his course. Then, with the island dissappearing behind him, he let himself relax. "Shit!" he said. "I don't need no more of that kind of fun. I feel like the house cat fucking the skunk. I ain't had all I want, just all I can stand."

But it was wasted on the girl. He could hear her crying in the back seat. He turned. She was huddled up in a mass of skirt and hair and doubled-up knees. He said, "It's all right. You can climb up here now."

She sobbed, "I think I'm going to be sick."

He said, "Goddammit, it's all over with. Quit the crying and get up here in the front seat."

It took her some time to compose herself enough to crawl into the right hand seat. She was still crying, sobbing quietly. China said, "Will you stop that, for God's sake."

She burst out afresh. She said, "This is a nightmare. I thought I would die. I've never been so scared in my life."

He said with disgust, "Pull yourself together, lady. Crying ain't helping you none, and it's driving me nuts."

They were flying about twenty feet above the waves.

She looked out the side window and turned back into the airplane, shuddering. She said, "Please don't be so close! Please. I have never flown in a small plane before."

Holding the wheel with his left hand, he got out a cigarette and lit it. Then he said, "Listen, lady, I have just stolen an airplane. I have also just killed a man back there on that airfield. I ain't guilty of anything that can't be straightened out, but the authorities would love to get their hands on me. I got enough of a start that a chase plane will have a hell of a time catching me before I get us to Miami. But there is radar. I don't know how low they read, but I ain't taking no chances. Got it? I want to get this son-of-a-bitch to Miami, then get on a commercial flight to Texas. After that I'll get things sorted out."

She peered out the window again, putting her fist to her mouth. "But it makes me so afraid. We are so close to the water. What should we do if something happens? If the motor quits?"

He cleared his throat. "There is a procedure for that. An emergency procedure. Would you like to have it explained so that you'll know what to do?"

"Oh yes," she said, "Please."

He said, "All right. If there is an emergency, if the engine quits, if something happens that is going to force us down, here is what you should do. You should sit as upright in your seat as you can. Then pull your seat belt as tight as you can. After that open you legs."

"Open my legs?"

"Yes. Open your legs. As wide as you can."

"Like this?"

"Yes, that's very good."

"Then next?"

"Then, from that position, you bend down and kiss your ass good-bye."

She was silent a moment, putting her knuckles to her

mouth and sobbing a little. Then she said, from her tear-streaked face, "Why would you tell me such a joke? Why are you so cruel to me?"

"Because I don't like you," China said matter-of-factly. He looked over at her. "I know you, darlin', know you very well. You're a beautiful girl and you been a beautiful girl for a long time. And you figure that's enough. When the beauty wasn't enough, when old John recovered his senses and ran out on you, you turned on him like a mad dog. Could have gotten him killed. I don't blame him. I'd of left you too. You're so fucking spoiled that you've got to where you believe the world owes you a living just because you're good-looking. Well, that ain't the way it works. I got a woman in Texas that is twice as good-looking as you and about three thousand times more a woman, and all you are to me is a delay getting back to her. You wouldn't make a spot on her ass. And the sooner you realize it and the sooner you get a little character going, the better off you're going to be. You can't pay your dues in life with just looks. The price is higher than that."

She looked down at her hands clenched in her lap, and didn't say a word.

Chapter Eleven

He hit the coast of Florida early in the evening, flying low and then climbing for altitude. As low as he'd been, he'd had to fly without benefit of electronic navigational aids and he was pleased he'd hit so close to Miami. But he had to climb to pick up a VOR vector that would direct him to the small airport where Cliff Finch had his fixed base operations business.

The girl had been silent for some time. But as he turned on heading toward the airport, she said, "What am I supposed to do now?"

He didn't answer her, just kept his attention on the ADF heading he was using to lead him to the airport. After a few moments more of flying he lined up on the active runway and landed in the growing twilight. He had called in on the Unicom and there was a flight line boy there to direct him to a parking place. He parked, turned off all the radio gear and then killed the engine with the mixture control. After that he got out of the airplane, helped the girl out, handed her her suitcase, and started walking toward the office of the flight service station. The girl was just behind him, her high heels sounding on the pavement of the taxiway. He thought idly that the girl's shoes could have gotten them both killed. And that she'd never had sense enough to take them off.

He pushed through the door of the office, his flight kit in his hand, the revolver still stuck in his belt under his shirt. Cliff Finch was leaning over the counter as he came in, a sour look on his face. The operator said, "Well, friends, he comes back here without my airplane, in one he stole, and he's got a girl with him. What am I supposed to think?"

There was no one else in the lounge except a couple of line boys. But China held up his hand. "Save it, buddy," he said. "Let's go in your office." He turned to the girl and pointed at a chair in the corner. "Sit over there," he said. "I won't be long."

Finch came around the counter and led the way down a hall to his office. He opened the door and let China precede him, saying, "This had better be good. But knowing you, I know it will be. You ain't never disappointed me yet."

China sat down and finally began to relax. What he mainly wanted was a beer, but he knew Finch wouldn't have any. He said, "You got any whiskey?"

The operator had gone behind his desk and sat down. He said, "Yeah. Bourbon. That all right?"

"Do I have a choice?"

"No."

"Then hand me the bottle."

"We got some plastic cups out there. I could put some ice in one."

"Hell with that. I'm in a hurry."

Finch opened a drawer and took out a bottle of Old Granddad. He handed it across to China.

China said, "Thanks." He unscrewed the cap and took a long pull of the hot, burning liquor. "Shit!" he said, taking the bottle from his mouth. "Whew!" He shook his head. "Do you people really like this stuff? Jesus H. Christ! Like Player says, I don't know whether to drink it or use it for paint thinner."

Finch was leaning back in his desk chair. He had lit a cigar. He said, "I reckon it is a little too strong for you Texas cowboys. Y'all ought to stick to mother's milk."

"If I'd had one," China said, "I might have." The bourbon had burned its way down and was beginning to spread and relax him. He leaned back and lit a cigarette. He said, "I suppose you've already heard a few things."

"Heard?" Finch leaned forward. "I don't guess you were monitoring any radio channels on the way back."

"No," China admitted, "I wasn't. I was already a little low in spirit and I didn't want to hear anything that might make me feel worse. Were they talking about me?"

"Not by name," Finch said. "They ain't on to that yet. But I knew it was you as soon as I heard the identification numbers on my Aztec. Where, by the way, *is* my airplane?"

"Cliff, your airplane is all right. Basically."

"Basically?"

"Yeah, basically." China leaned forward. "Now be quiet. I want to tell you what I need and what we can do. Your airplane is safe and sound in Fujardo. All it's got is a bullet through the windscreen." He paused. "Actually, there were a lot of bullets flying around and it may have been hit more than once. I don't know. But whatever the damage is, we'll pay for it." He reached in his pocket and pulled out a set of keys. "There's the keys. Go and get it. It ought to still be sitting right there. When you come up with the final bill, let the man in New York know and

we'll pay. Next is the matter of the airplane I flew here
in."

"Oh yeah. You mean the one you stole."

"That's a little harsh, Cliff. Let's just call it the airplane
that I needed at the time. I want you to find out who owns
it. Get it back to him and give him, oh, say, five hundred
dollars for his trouble. Assure him that his plane is better
now than it was for having been flown by the great China
Blue."

Finch said, "Oh shit, do I have to listen to this?"

"Yes. Lay it on thick. I think you maybe can save me
some trouble if you yourself take the plane back and
explain what was going down to the ol' boy that I jerked
out of the plane at pistol point. Right now I imagine he's a
little upset."

Finch said dryly, "I just feel plumb privileged to do
these things for the great China Blue."

"Now don't be sarcastic. I ain't got the time. I want to
get home to Texas." He picked up the bottle of bourbon
by his chair and took another drink. He did not grimace so
badly the second time. He said, "This is all going to get
straightened out. And you'll get your money, which is all
you care about. Now I want two last things."

"I hope neither one of them things is going to involve
another one of my airplanes."

"No. I want your office for a few moments. That girl
out there is about to need to make a phone call. After that I
want one of your boys to drive me to the international
airport. I'm going back to Texas tonight."

Finch got up. He said, "It's sure my pleasure to know
my office is going to be used by the great China Blue. And
think what a thrill it's going to be for one of my boys to
get to drive the great China Blue to the airport. They'll
probably wish later they'd been keeping a diary. Just to
record the event."

China said, "Go to hell, Finch. You're just dying of envy."

Ugette was sitting on a small leatherette couch, staring out the big window that faced onto the flight line. She looked very bedraggled and wrinkled and frightened. China sat down beside her and lit a cigarette. She turned her strained face toward him. He said, "Ugette, do you know how to reach John by phone?"

She nodded numbly.

He said, "I mean now, after business hours? At home?"

She nodded again. "Yes." She touched her purse which was still slung over her shoulder. "I have his number in here."

He pointed. "Down that hall, the first door on the left, is an office. Go in there and call him. Warn him what has happened and what might happen. See what he says to you."

She said, "I am to call him now?"

He nodded. "Yes, now. I don't have much time. Make it snappy."

"But I won't know what to say!"

He drew on his cigarette. "Ugette, I am getting damn tired of your little-girl act. A man's life could be in danger. Just tell him that. You ought to have brains enough to handle that."

She got up and he watched her as she went down the hall toward the office. Finch had come to stand behind the little counter in the lounge. He was looking at China. He raised his eyebrows. "How do you manage to get yourself is so much trouble?" he asked.

"Just lucky, I guess."

The line boys had disappeared, and the lounge was quiet. The operator said, "You know I got to report that stolen aircraft landing here."

"Of course I know it, you fat cracker. But you give me

two or three hours to get the hell out of here. I'll handle everything from Texas.''

Finch said, ''I took the liberty of calling the airlines. The great China Blue has got a reservation on a flight out of here in about an hour and a half. However, I am happy to tell you, you'll have a layover in Atlanta and won't get into Austin until the small hours of the morning. I hope you feel like shit when you get there.''

''You are one of the great human beings of all time, Finch.''

''I just try to help when I can. I spend my life plugging holes in the dam for my fellow man.''

''If I could have you rendered into lard, I'd be a rich man.''

''And if I could buy you for what you're worth and sell you for what you think you're worth, I'd also be a rich man.''

Out of the corner of his eye China saw the girl come out of the office and down the hall. He motioned with his head. ''Get out of here. I got to talk privately.''

''Of course, Mister Blue, of course.''

The girl came in, her head down, and sat on the couch beside him. He said, ''Well?''

She didn't answer.

He said, ''Did you get him? Did you get him on the phone?''

She sat there, her eyes downcast. She was crying again.

He said, ''Listen, I ain't going to ask you again. Did you get him on the phone?''

After a long pause she said, ''Yes. He answered. I could hear his children in the background.''

''So? Did you tell him!''

She was a long time in answering. She said, ''Yes. He thought it was a trick.'' She began to cry. ''He said never to call him at home again. He did not believe me.''

He got out a cigarette and lit it. The lounge seemed very quiet. He said, "Then that's his lookout. You warned him. That's all you can do."

She was still crying. She said, "But what am I to do? I thought he would be grateful. I thought he would come and take care of me. What is to become of me?"

He said, "You must have credit cards. You can use one of them to get a ticket on an airplane back to Columbia."

She was still crying.

"No, I have nothing. They took everything from me back in Fujardo."

He got his billfold out of his back pocket and took two hundred dollars out. He held it out to her. She looked at it uncertainly. "Here," he sighed. "take it. You can use it to get home."

Chapter Twelve

They were sitting around the breakfast table when the phone rang. He was barefoot and barebacked in just a pair of easy-feeling jeans. Bonnie was sitting across from him, in her slit-down-the-sides Oriental robe, working the crossword puzzle. He was drinking a Coke and reading the *Wall Street Journal*. He did not glance up when the phone rang. It rang several times and she said, "Oh, hell!", and got up and went into the den to answer it. In a moment she was back. She said, "It's him. Go and talk."

He went into the den, lit a cigarette and then, after a moment, picked up the receiver. "Yeah," he said, "tell me how much trouble I'm in."

He talked for five minutes and then he went back into the kitchen and sat down and picked up his paper and started reading again.

She waited a long time. He could see it working on her. Finally she said, "All right, China, now tell me, dammit! Are we going to jail?"

He turned a page and looked at her. "What are you talking about, woman?"

"You bastard! What's the deal?"

"Oh," he said "Oh, that." He put the paper down. "No, it's all straightened out. The guy whose plane I borrowed is totally cooled out. The police have been enlightened through our contacts in San Juan, and there are more than a few public servants who are quite pleased to have Señor Cortez out of commission. Cliff is all paid off and everyone is satisfied. I may not even lose my pilot's license over the whole thing. What do you think of that?"

She looked at him a long moment, her golden blond hair surrounding her face. She said, "I think you are the luckiest son-of-a-bitch in the world. How you get away with it I'll never know."

He said, "You get a hold of Jane? Do she and Player know we'll be down in a couple of days to spend some time?"

"Yes, they know."

He suddenly made a sour face. "The profit, net, off of this whole fucking business is barely three thousand dollars. What do you think of that?"

She said, "You're home alive, aren't you?"

"I always expect to get home alive. Hell, I'm good at what I do."

She said, "When are you going to retire? Cut out this foolishness?"

"Oh, soon," he said. "Very soon."

She said, "You are lying. You are lying in your teeth."

He had picked the paper back up and was reading it. He said, "You are probably right."

She said, "Listen, I know about the money. But what I want to know is what kind of payment did you get from those two women whose asses you saved?"

He put the paper down and looked up at her. "What are you talking about?"

She said, "Don't kid me. You told me straight about pulling two females out of deep and serious trouble. I know you and I know that was the truth. Now I want to know how they paid you back."

He said, "Bonnie, now come on! You know better than that."

She said, "Tell me, you bastard."

"I will tell you the truth," he said. "I was no more intimate with either one of those young ladies than I have been with my banker. The one gave me a kiss of thanks just the same as a man would shake my hand if I'd done him a good turn."

"You swear?"

"I swear," he said.

She slipped out of her chair and knelt on her knees beside him. She put her hand up and ran it over his furry chest and over the ragged scar from the one bad plane crash he'd had. She said, "Dammit, when are you going to marry me?"

He said, "When I quit being a venture pilot."

"Then when are you going to tell me where you got that crazy name?"

"Never," he said, "Because then you'd think I was a social misfit and you wouldn't love me as much."

She reached up, suddenly, fiercely, and took him by the sides of his face. She said, "Dammit, China Blue, I love you."

Outside, in the cold of the November morning, his blaze-faced horse whinnied contentedly.